a novel

THE LAST SUMMER BEFORE WHATEVER HAPPENS NEXT

Also from Islandport Press

The Space Between You and Me
Julie True Kingsley

What the Wind Can Tell You
Sarah Marie Aliberti Jette

The Sugar Mountain Snow Ball
Elizabeth Atkinson

Mercy
Sarah L. Thomson

Uncertain Glory
Lea Wait

The Door to January
Gillian French

Billy Boy
Jean Mary Flahive

The Fog of Forgetting
G.A. Morgan

Chantarelle
G.A. Morgan

a novel

THE LAST SUMMER BEFORE WHATEVER HAPPENS NEXT

Bee Burke

Islandport Press

ISLANDPORT PRESS

Islandport Press
P.O. Box 10
Yarmouth, Maine 04096
www.islandportpress.com
info@islandportpress.com

First Edition: September 2024
Printed in the United States of America.

ISBN: 978-1-952143-82-3
Library of Congress Control Number: 2024935373

Dean L. Lunt | Editor-in-Chief, Publisher
Shannon M. Butler | Vice President
Emily A. Lunt | Book Designer
Marion F. Fearing | Assistant Editor
Cover art courtesy of Tarikdiz/Shutterstock

To Jodi Casey.

CHAPTER ONE

June 1980-Something

"Come on, they're catching us," I heard a girl's voice say. The next thing I knew, her arm was looped into mine, and she was pulling me down Water Street. I found myself running to keep up with her, trying hard not to trip over my long sundress.

I had never met this girl, but I knew who she was. Pepper Toohey. How did I know? Everyone knew who the Tooheys were. That family was one of the biggest, if not *the* biggest, manufacturers of plumbing supplies in North America. If you are reading this on the toilet, stand up and look around. Chances are it says *Toohey* on the tank.

Living in Keech, Maine, it was impossible not to know who they were. My dad thought the Tooheys were God's gift to the town. He loved telling Toohey stories. He loved hearing Toohey stories. Most people, however, thought they were just stuck-up snobs that clogged the best seats in the restaurants in the summer and hogged the best parts of the coast for themselves.

Pepper's dad was the big boss at the toilet company, and she was the big boss of her cousins. We had both just graduated—her from some prep school in Massachusetts and me from Keech Town High. She was wearing crazy huge vintage sunglasses and a big floppy hat. Her blonde hair was pulled into two pigtails. I didn't know anyone my age who still wore pigtails, but on Pepper, it somehow looked all right. The sunglasses called attention to the spray of large freckles that spanned the bridge of her nose. They were pronounced and spread apart, like she had been Raggedy Ann for Halloween and never washed off the face paint. Come to think about it, that's how I recognized her.

I looked behind us, and a pack of her cousins were following us down Water Street past the dockside restaurants and souvenir shops. Pepper smacked her dime-store flip-flops as loud as she could as we rushed along the sidewalk speckled with gull poop. She was wearing a gray tank top, patched jeans, and a madras shirt, unbuttoned and untucked, as if thrown on as an afterthought. It fluttered behind her as she sped along.

She directed us into the Dock n' Dine just as they were opening. The Dock n' Dine was the town's best restaurant, and it had the best summer jobs—boaters too drunk to sail, showing off for each other with outrageous tips. I had never worked there. Our housekeeper, Flo, told Dad the waitresses there get groped—and "those girls" encouraged it to get bigger tips. After that, the Dock n' Dine was completely off-limits for me—even for dinner. And that was a bummer because it used to be our special occasion restaurant. The last time we came here, it was because I got a 1260 on my PSATs. And now, here I was with the Tooheys on some random Tuesday in June.

We were greeted with dirty looks from some of my class-mates—well, they weren't my classmates anymore. They were waitstaff now—maybe forever. Pepper moved the CLOSED sign out of a section and commandeered a large dockside table. The rest of the family caught up and began to settle around the table. She quickly pushed me down into a chair next to the tallest—and cutest—boy in the group. I guessed he was her brother, Pike. She sat on the other side of me.

When everyone was finally seated, Pepper snapped her head around and looked at me.

"Wait a minute, who the hell are you?" she said.

CHAPTER TWO

Why would she know who I was? What was I even doing there with these people?

I should have been working somewhere like I did every summer. But Dad had other plans. He wanted me to have a "summer of freedom" before college, and so, this was the first time I could even remember having nothing to do—no summer job, not even babysitting. I always worked June and July and then spent all of August at enrichment camps, one right after the other. Not fun-in-the-sun camps—camps with a purpose like foreign language or tennis or theater. That was okay; I liked it that way.

He cooked up this idea as a graduation present to me. He gave me a certificate that he had made at work and gave it to me in a card, right after graduation when we were having carrot cake at home. The cake was too big, as usual, since there were just the four of us. Me and Dad, Flo and her girlfriend, Ebbie. I was the only person there without gray hair and sensible shoes.

There had been one wrapped present and two cards. Inside the little box was a pair of small gold hoop earrings from Flo and

Ebbie. They looked like bookends, sitting there on the couch in their khaki Bermuda shorts and crisply ironed pastel plaid blouses.

There was a card from Mom and her new husband—sorry they couldn't make it, here's a check. And the card from Dad with the certificate. It said:

MY PRESENT TO YOU IS THE SUMMER OFF. NO WORK.
NO HEAVY READING. NO ENRICHMENT CAMPS. ONE SUMMER
OF FREEDOM BEFORE COLLEGE.

LOVE, DAD

Oh crap. I didn't want that. Cash would have been so much better.

"Thanks, Dad, but I better get a job before all the good ones are taken. I don't want to end up folding T-shirts," I told him.

I liked having a plan and a schedule. I liked my days to be filled with tasks and to-dos, and I liked the sense of accomplishment in checking them off. I had actually memorized the menu from the Captain's Catch already, figuring that would be the second-best place to work after the forbidden Dock n' Dine.

"You just hang out and enjoy yourself this summer," he said. Clueless. He looked clueless, too, having worn a suit and tie to a graduation ceremony where everyone else wore their best shirt-sleeves. I felt weird enough without him showing up, making everyone nervous like he's there to do an audit.

I didn't know how to just hang out due to a lack of experience. They didn't teach that at enrichment camps, and I wasn't exactly popular. The kids in Keech were nice enough to me—especially if they needed homework help or a shift covered. But I never sat on top of the picnic tables at Dairy Dip with them, smashed bottles at the dump, or encouraged seagulls to poop on tourists' cars by feeding them oyster crackers at the pier.

"I've put money away for this. I'll give you a weekly allowance. Not a lot, but enough for some fun. You've worked your tail off every summer. You'll be busy enough this fall in college. You've earned this," he said.

"That's true, you did," Flo backed him up.

"She's always worked hard," chimed Ebbie.

"And look what we have now. Class valedictorian, with her picture in the paper," Dad said.

"Just the *Keech Town Crier*. It's mostly ads," I grumbled.

"It was the front page!" Ebbie said.

"Yeah, right next to a story about the mountain lion turd."

"That's big news!" Flo said.

"Game warden says that's a load of hooey," Dad said.

"I believe it. There's all kinds of stuff out here. Stuff like you wouldn't believe," Flo said. Flo believed in Bigfoot. A mountain lion on the loose in Keech was somehow Bigfoot evidence for her.

"And a full ride in the fall. A full ride!" Dad said, steering the subject away from Bigfoot before it got there.

"If anyone has earned a summer off, it's you, Claire," Flo said.

My graduation "party" ended with Flo and Ebbie driving home on their scooter and Dad falling asleep on the couch. My classmates were at real parties. The sort that goody two-shoes, smarty-pants valedictorians don't get invited to. Which was just as well. I knew I would hate those parties. But sometimes, it would have been nice just to be asked.

With no homework, nothing to study for, no reason to go to bed early, no camp to prepare for, no job to fill the hours, I suddenly felt overwhelmingly lonely. Maybe I had always been and was just too busy to notice. The house was quiet with only Dad's snores and the hum of the refrigerator. No breeze swayed the pines outside; no cars drove by. Somewhere in the woods or down on a beach, my classmates were having a bonfire. I didn't even know where it was, and no one had thought to include me.

I faced a whole summer of that.

I knew it sounded ungrateful. Some people save up and wait all year to spend a week by the sea in Maine. But to be clear, we didn't live down in Keech Harbor, the cute seaside village. We lived in Keech Town, just a few miles inland and across the state highway, which made a world of difference. In Keech Town, there's nothing but pine forests and the occasional moose. And Keech Harbor itself is so far up the coast that most tourists can't be bothered with it. We get just enough to keep us busy over summer. The Tooheys and a handful of other rich families have massive summer "cottages" just outside the village along Hazard Point, the rocky curve of land that protects the harbor.

We lived in Keech because it's where my dad was from. We lived on the same land that's been in our family since 1750. So you couldn't get my dad out of Keech even if you blew it up. My mother certainly tried.

Mom hated Keech so much that she moved to Boston. At first, it was for work, but then it turned out to be for a man she worked with. She's in finance. She earns big bucks. Dad's an accountant, a bean counter. My mother says he counts other people's money instead of making his own. Even so, that made us pretty fancy for Keech Town, which was another reason I never fit in. Too rich to be a townie, too poor for the Harbor crowd.

I guess that's why I always dreamed of getting on the highway and driving away. Except I never bought a car. Or learned how to drive. That's why Dad had to drop me off in Keech Harbor on that first day of my "summer of freedom."

I stood there alone, like a disoriented tourist, at the far end of Water Street by Milfred's Mini Golf, the Dairy Dip, and Java Bubbles Launderette and Coffee Shoppe. Water Street's signage read like my resume.

Souvenir shops lined one side of Water Street. That's what I did the summer before I was old enough to officially work. One of my dad's friends paid me under the table for a few hours if I helped her tidy the place up once a week—folding T-shirts and poking a feather duster along the rows of snow globes, shot glasses, and paperweights. Who needed a paperweight? It's amazing the kind of junk people buy on vacation.

Then there's the market and post office before you get into the thick of it—the tiny beach, the waterfront restaurants: The Lucky Lobster, Keech House of Pizza (every town I've ever been to seemed to have a House of Pizza), the Captain's Catch, the Dock n' Dine. Further down, Water Street turns into Hazard Point Road, and then it dead-ends with the big houses of the Toohey compound and the lighthouse.

I sat on a bench by the dock, reading in the morning sun. Bird-watchers were lining up for a boat ride to see the many islands that dot the harbor. It was supposed to be one of the best places for bird-watching on the East Coast. I didn't know; I had been to Audubon camp, but I'd never been out on the water.

Dad also didn't want me reading serious books that summer. He had a lady at work pick out some light reading for me. He came home with a flowery novel, and I took its book jacket off and wrapped it around whichever book it fit that was on my reading list for the fall, which happened to be *Macroeconomics 101*. After I read a chapter, I took a walk down Water Street. Maybe I'd go to the library once they opened. Maybe I'd apply for a job somewhere.

In the window at the souvenir shop, I could see a girl I knew from gym class folding T-shirts. She had just finished folding a pile when she knocked the pile next to it over with her elbow. *Dummy.*

My prom date, Tim, waved from the boat with the bird watchers. What a great job for him. He was going to study marine biology in the fall. Even though he was a real nerd, he fit in, unlike me, because his older brother was a football hero and his dad was a cop. He's a lifer. He'd go away to study marine biology all right, but he'd come back to Keech, no doubt about that. He told me on prom night that we were destined to be together. I thought not. I knew for a fact that as soon as he dropped me at home, he took off to one of those bonfires without me.

Steve from the House of Pizza called out to me from the side door. He'd been working at his parents' pizza place since I was able to see over the counter.

"Hey you, slacker! No job today? Get in here, and start tossing salad."

"I'm not working this summer," I said to him.

"What? Oh, I get it! The big fancy valedictorian is too good for work now?" he shouted. I could never tell if he was joking or flirting.

I kept walking . . . and then the next thing I knew, I was at the Dock n' Dine, sitting at a table full of Tooheys, who were staring at me and demanding to know why I was there.

CHAPTER THREE

"I'm Claire Hart," I answered, maybe confessed, to Pepper Toohey and the table full of her fair-haired relations staring at me.

"You grabbed her off the street and dragged her in here!" the tall boy next to me shouted in my defense.

He brushed his long bangs out of his eyes. His hair was that dark, pre-summer blond that was sure to lighten in the sun. He was thin, but not skinny. He was wearing a faded T-shirt that said *Nantucket*. If he was Pike, then he would probably be a sophomore in college.

"What? I'm sorry. I thought she was your new girlfriend, Pike," Pepper said in a loud stage whisper. It was the most insincere apology I had ever heard.

"I'm his new girlfriend!" a brunette, seated at the far end of the table, declared as she stood up, copying his tone and gesture, except she had no bangs to brush back.

Her hair was perfectly contained behind a navy blue headband embroidered with little sailboats. Of course she was Pike's girlfriend.

She was beautifully dressed; she wore a short white dress and navy blue sandals, both patterned with the same sailboats on her head. I felt like a ragamuffin sitting there in my old sundress and beat-up sandals, even though the Toohey kids all looked like bums, too.

The girlfriend was impeccably groomed. I had taken a shower that morning, but this girl just glowed.

"Oops. Sorry. My mistake," Pepper said. "Can't seem to keep them straight."

"I should get going," I said and stood. I could feel my face turning red and throbbing in humiliation.

Pepper pulled me back down.

"No way. You have to stay for lunch—that is, if you're free. Please let me make up for my rudeness. We're here almost every day in summer; we were bound to meet and be friends sooner or later. Why not today?" She said it with a big smile.

Ha. That's a joke. I had lived in Keech my whole entire life, and I had never actually met a live Toohey before. I had waited on some at the Dairy Dip two summers ago. But despite the fact that my dad knew her dad and that every summer, the town swelled with Tooheys migrating to their family compound, I couldn't say I had ever officially met one.

"Oh, please stay!" the girl across from me said. "Pepper's right. We were bound to meet sooner or later. And now we have a great how-we-met story!"

"Yeah, you can be the friend Pepper kidnapped," Pike said, and they all laughed.

"Yes, we're going to hold you for ransom," Pepper joked, and they all laughed again.

I weighed my options. Since it would be slightly less embarrassing to stay and have lunch than get up and walk away with kids from school watching, I stayed.

"Yes, why not today?" I said, and they all cheered. No other introductions were made. The Tooheys just assumed everyone knew who they were. The sad thing was I did kinda know who they all were, if not specifically than by tradition. Every generation had its confusing array of juniors and a Pike and a Pepper and a Pixie and a Cheddar. So basically, if you guessed from that selection of nicknames, no matter how old you were, at least one of them in your own age range would answer.

A girl from school waited on us and pretended not to know me. This was good, since Pepper ordered a beer for herself and one for me, although clearly none of us were old enough to drink. But the drinks came anyway. I would never have tried that here—or anyplace else for that matter.

I put my tote bag under the table, and it fell over, sending my book sliding onto the feet of the girl across from me. She picked it up and placed it on the table in front of her, then pulled a pair of vintage round tortoiseshell eyeglasses from her purse and read the jacket.

"Oh I love this author!" she said. *Please don't open that*, I prayed. The girl turned it over and examined the back. Her blonde hair was cut into a 1920s-style bob with severe bangs. A bumblebee barrette was clipped into her hair on the left side of her head, serving absolutely no purpose other than to sparkle.

This would have to be Pixie. She shared her nickname with a kooky great-aunt who lived alone on one of the harbor islands and wrote poetry and letters of outrage, both of which she sent into the *Keech Town Crier*. I always thought Pixie was a lot younger than me, but here she was, drinking beer with the rest of us. I had seen her around town all year, mostly at the bookstore and the post office, wearing her trademark red sneakers and retro eyeglasses. If she ever noticed me, she certainly didn't let on. She was the only cousin whose family lived in Keech Harbor year-round. She didn't go to a fancy prep school. She was homeschooled or, as she put it, "tutored." I wish I had known that was legal to do. I would have liked to spend a few years at home reading books and keeping Flo company while she cleaned.

She handed the book back to me, and I slipped my disguised textbook back into the bag.

"Split a bucket of steamers, Meredith?" Pike called over to the girlfriend, who was resigned to her seat in exile at the far end of the table. She whipped her head toward him, flipping her brown hair and shooting him a look.

"Gross," she said.

"How about you?" he said to me. "Would you split a bucket with me?"

I said yes, even though I had a sandwich in my tote bag that I would have to eat later because Flo made it and would want to know why I didn't eat it. It didn't occur to me that I could feed it to the gulls instead.

The clams were messy but good. The only conversation I had with Pike involved the quality of individual clams ("good one" or "sandy"), the butter, and the discard dish for the shells. Still, Meredith, the girlfriend, didn't like it. Listening to every word, she sat still, fork in hand and poised motionless over a plate of iceberg lettuce and rigid cherry tomatoes (who orders salad at the Dock n' Dine?), waiting for an opportunity to stick that fork in my eye.

I never knew clams could be so threatening! I got them because I figured splitting a bucket of clams would be the cheapest option.

But that didn't matter, because the bill never came. The Tooheys just got up and took me with them. I reached for my purse, but Pepper stopped me.

"Don't worry about it; it's all on Uncle Chet's tab," she whispered. "He's taking us for a sail this afternoon—you should come! It will be so much fun! I just love the first sail of the season . . . And don't thank him for lunch, whatever you do," she said, winked, and then laughed.

Dad said he wanted me to have fun this summer. And here I was about to go sailing with the Tooheys. How could he object to that? He thought they were God's gift to Keech. So I went.

CHAPTER FOUR

We walked back through the village toward the town dock where Chet Toohey's massive yacht, the *Plunger*, waited. Pepper and I were up front, followed by Pike and his girlfriend, now clinging to his side like a barnacle. They'd have to scrape her off with a putty knife before she'd get separated from him again. Behind us, Pixie walked with a chubby redheaded boy. Two other cousins said goodbye and headed back to the house. They were from the Connecticut branch of the family.

The *Plunger* dwarfed every other boat in Keech Harbor. It was usually moored at the Dock n' Dine, with Chet Toohey moored inside at the bar. But today, it sat waiting for us at the end of the pier, its masts towering above the smattering of boats that bobbed along beside it.

"Welcome aboard," a man said to me. He was tall and broad-shouldered, which offset his giant beer belly so well you almost didn't notice it. His hair was a weird color somewhere between blond and gray, and his face was bright with wicked bad rosacea, blossoms of red covering his cheeks. My dad had a touch of it, and he was always yelling at me to wear sunscreen and showing me pictures of worst-case scenarios—and this guy was a textbook case. This had to be Pepper's Uncle Chet. Pepper introduced us.

"Oh, you're Paul Hart's girl, the valedictorian. Congratulations, well done! Paul's a grand fellow. Good to have you aboard, Claire. Just a grand fellow, your dad. We picked blueberries together as kids."

How well I knew. That was one of Dad's favorite Toohey stories. He had worked with Chet—they called him Cheddar then—and with one of the Pikes—Pepper's dad—one summer up on the blueberry barrens.

"Our generation, we learned to work hard, so you kids wouldn't have to," he said, patting me on the back.

I couldn't wait to tell Dad I now had one of my own Toohey stories. And that he worked hard so I wouldn't have to. There it was—his theme for my summer spoken by a Toohey!

"Have you met my son, Cheddar?" he asked, pointing to the doughy redhead.

The boy smiled, showing rows of tiny teeth that, with his copious collection of freckles, made him look like a jack-o'-lantern.

I smiled back and then had to quickly defend my crotch as a little black dog rested its paws on my knee and sniffed me in the most embarrassing way. I gently directed it away and patted its head.

"Please don't mind that dog. It's my mother's. She used to breed German Shepherds—I swear some of those dogs could read. Then she went and fell in love with this foolish creature—the only Schipperke in the world who's afraid of the water. Aren't you,

you little dope? Dumb thing sinks like a stone," he said, patted the dog on its head, and excused himself.

"Pepper, I don't know anything about sailing," I confessed as I pulled her in close enough to whisper. She answered loud enough for everyone to hear.

"That's okay. It's better to be honest and say so than try to fake it, fall overboard, and need the Coast Guard to come rescue you, right, Meredith?" Pepper said.

"It was only the harbormaster, Pep, jeez," Pike said.

Pepper smiled at me and lifted her eyebrows a couple of times like we had a private joke. But then she took me aside and whispered, "Don't worry about it, we won't be under sail. Uncle Chet hardly ever sets the sails on the *Plunger*."

We motored out into Keech Harbor, cruising around its dozens of motley islands and finally mooring in a sheltered south-facing cove on one of the bigger ones. This island was tall, like it might have been part of a headland once upon a time (geology camp fun fact). Most were insignificant—so small they didn't even warrant a name—and some had names, but they disappeared at king tides, leaving just a few scraggly pines poking out of the water. Some were just seal haul-outs. This island was one of the three biggest in Keech Harbor.

There was Pregnant Island. My dad told me it was named this because of its shape, but Flo said it was where young girls went to ruin their lives and that I had better never, ever go there in a million years.

Little Rest Island was where the kooky Toohey aunt lived. You can only reach it by a causeway that appears at low tide. She kept a car in her garage on the side of the road near the causeway and timed her grocery runs so she could haul her groceries out to Little Rest in a child-sized red wagon.

And then the biggest was this one, where we moored. It was Alden Island on the map, but the Tooheys called it Mount Saint Picnic.

It looked like all the others from the shore—chunky granite lumps crowned with pines. But Alden Island was shaped like a crescent, and the inner curve, hidden from view from town, held a rare sandy beach. It was tiny as beaches go, maybe just the size of our house, but it shimmered with a natural blanket of soft sand, nestled in the curves of the cove.

The Tooheys had a little skiff and a mooring for the *Plunger* just offshore. Cheddar piloted the skiff and took Pepper, Pixie, and me ashore in it to the sandy beach. He dropped us off and returned for Pike, Meredith, and his dad. The dog yipped until it was clear she was being left on the boat and then went below to sleep.

I had heard a story that the Tooheys owned an island in the harbor with a secret beach with the warmest waters in New England. I thought it was just a story, like the one where they said the Tooheys kept a crazy cousin locked up in the lighthouse. They said you could see the lights inside the vacant old keeper's quarters at night, but I never saw them.

But the thing about the water turned out to be true. The saucer-shaped cove was shallow and sandy. At low tide, the sun beat against the sand, and in turn, the hot sand heated the returning water. Usually, the bay is numbingly cold in August. Here, it was only June, and the water was pleasant enough to wade into up to your shins. It was like I had stepped into some fairytale version of my own town. I followed Pepper's lead and kicked my shoes off and waded along the shore.

Cheddar leapt out of the skiff, causing a big splash that wet and annoyed Meredith. He secured the skiff to a tree that grew out over the water. Pike helped him pull it up onto the sand and then had to carry Meredith until she determined they were far up the beach enough for her to touch the ground.

Cheddar opened a little shed on the beach, and out came a few pieces of ancient lawn furniture, a camp table, and a wooden crate of what I guess you could call their beach toys: a cribbage set, some pails, nets for harassing minnows. Cheddar set up the furniture. Pixie sat down and tried to organize a cribbage game; Cheddar was her only taker. Meredith and Pike made out in the hammock. Uncle Chet fell fast asleep on a rickety chaise, his hat balanced on his face to shield it from the sun. I kept expecting the chaise to collapse. But it stood strong while Uncle Chet snored away on top of it, the ancient, musty canvas straps straining against the wooden frame.

"Who wants to hike around the island?" Pepper asked.

Meredith whispered a "no" to Pike, and he relayed their answer.

"Come on," Pepper said to me. It didn't occur to me that I had a choice. I just went because she told me to. We put our shoes on and followed a footpath that led away from the beach and up to where the island exposed its rocky heart, over tangled knots of pine roots and along treacherous patches of poison ivy.

"Hate this stuff!" Pepper shouted at the vines and whacked their shiny leaves of three with a fallen branch. I jumped back and lost my footing. But she grabbed me with her other hand and dropped the branch.

"Sorry. I hope that's the only patch of it. Gran's gardener came out here last year and got rid of most of it."

Neither of us were wearing the right shoes for hiking, and even though a hike around the entire island couldn't be much more than a half a mile, the trail was still difficult and steep, rocky in some spots and sandy and unreliable in others.

Pepper pointed out small red berries—juneberries, –she called them—and told me to try them. I did and hoped she knew what she was talking about. But she ate a handful, too. They were tart, nothing special—the sort of thing that once upon a time, people were probably grateful for after a long winter, like fiddleheads. Fiddleheads are gross. My grandmother gathered, cooked, and made us eat them every spring, served up with heaping piles of fiddlehead stories—where to find them, how to cook them, and how delicious they are. Maybe they were—after a long winter during the Great Depression. In retrospect, I wonder if she cooked those ferns just to piss my mother off.

The trail turned inward to the center of the island, and we reached its bare bedrock top. I had climbed places like this before. They're everywhere around here—rocky outcrops that were fun to climb and rewarded those that did with great views. But unlike every other trail like this I had ever been on, there was not one piece of litter—not one broken bottle or beer cap or tangled nest of fishing line. It was pristine. And it gave me a view of Keech I had never seen before.

Stepping onto the highest part of it, we could see all of the village—the entire arc from the cliffs at Black Point to the Toohey compound and lighthouse on Hazard Point.

Hazard Point was the name of the rocky peninsula that curved around Keech Harbor like a protective arm, like the next bay over was trying to copy its paper. The sprawling Toohey colony sitting atop Hazard Point's dark cliffs and the recently decommissioned lighthouse provided the picture-perfect backdrop that made people cough up twice as much as they should for a plate of fried fish. You could even get a view of it on a postcard, flapping flags and all. It was a far cry from the factory in the shabby mill town where they made toilets and pipes and tanks and all kinds of other shitty things, miles and miles inland and down the coast.

"Cool view, huh?" Pepper said. "We used to always walk up here together. It's part of a visit to the island. Part of the reason we come here. Gran says it's good to get another perspective on things. Now, Pixie and Cheddar are too lazy, and Pike does whatever Meredith tells him to. I'm really glad you were game or I'd be sitting up here getting another perspective all by myself. It's not much of a hike, though," she said, yanking a pinecone off a twisted tree branch and winging it over the treetops. For a moment, I considered what would happen to it—would it float somewhere and grow, choke a fish that tried to eat it, or sink to the bottom and die unfulfilled?

We stood at the summit and looked around. Keech Harbor seemed silent. Occasionally, I could make out a little motion along Water Street if a big truck went by. From the island, it was like the streets had disappeared. It looked static, like a Christmas village inside a souvenir snow globe. The buildings looked small and quaint. All those places I worked along Water Street—my entire employment history—would never matter outside the bubble of the village. There was no sign of the state highway; Keech Town, my high school, my house, the mountain lion, Bigfoot, and everything beyond the village disappeared into the trees along with the secret locations of those parties and bonfires I was never invited to. They were all just specks somewhere amid the pine forest.

Maybe her gran's right; it's good to get another perspective on things.

"Ready?" Pepper said. I guess that meant it was time to go. We crossed the island's rocky top and followed another trail down. By the time we got back to the beach, Cheddar had packed everything up, and in no time, we were back on the *Plunger*. We weighed anchor—a phrase I learned just then and there—and started our cruise back.

Then, with a bark, a scream, and a splash, the Schipperke went overboard and sank into the cold dark water. Without a thought, I dived over the side of the *Plunger* after her.

CHAPTER FIVE

Lucky for me, summer camp last year included lifeguard certification and cold-water rescue safety.

The frigid water shocked my system at first—especially since I half-expected it to be as warm as the cove. I felt my chest go numb and my heart race, but I knew it was key to stay calm and catch my breath. I really resented that dog, even though I found her quickly. She was panicked and did not want to be rescued. I held tight to her as she kicked against me, scratching my chest. I surfaced quickly, gasping for air as she dug her hind claws into my thighs. Cheddar threw me a life preserver, and then he and Pike pulled us toward the boat.

"Woo-hoo! Way to go, Flipper!" Uncle Chet yelled. Cheddar reached over and lifted up the dog, who wriggled and yipped until she was placed on the deck. Pike pulled me onto the boat, and Uncle Chet wrapped a towel around me.

"Atta girl!" he shouted.

"Way to go, Flipper!" Pepper yelled, wrapping her arm around me.

"Flipper to the rescue!" Pixie shouted. I wondered if that was going to be my nickname. They all had them. If you had a nickname, you were in.

I shivered so hard my teeth chattered. Jumping into that cold water was a really dumb thing to do. But that little dog! The whole episode lasted only minutes, but they fussed over me like I had been pulled from the wreckage of the *Titanic*.

"Get her down below," Uncle Chet said. "Pepper, find her something dry to wear. Some sweats or something. Pix, make her a cup of tea, warm but not hot, decaf. Pike, you've got the helm. Take us home," Uncle Chet cranked out orders, and his crew scurried.

"Don't look so smug," Meredith hissed into my ear as I walked by her. *Smug?* I was sure I looked like a drowned rat. "You don't get a nickname that fast."

Pepper escorted me down below and wrapped me in a wool blanket. Pretty soon, I was in dry clothes—baggy sweats from some Connecticut prep school. They were probably Cheddar's based on the size of them. Pixie handed me a mug of chamomile. Pepper wrung out my soggy clothes in the "head," another new nautical term for the day.

They coddled me all the way to Hazard Point. I was still swaddled in blankets when I returned to deck as we approached the Point. It was even more impressive from the sea than it was from shore. I watched as their private dock came into view. The path that led to the main house zigzagged up along the dark rocks and beach roses, interrupted here and there at the steepest points with a handrail or a cluster of stone steps. Over that, a bright green lawn rose up in terraces like a green wedding cake, topped with the cluster of clapboard mansions.

As soon as we docked, Uncle Chet barked out new orders.

"I'll drive you home, kiddo," he said to me. "Ched, Pike, you've got *Plunger* duty. Pix, Pep, clean the salt off that dog before your grandmother sees her. Meredith, Meredith?—what happened to your friend, Pike? Jeepus Crackers—we didn't lose her in the drink again?!"

"Nope, she's still with us. She ran up to the house to use the bathroom. She won't use the head on the *Plunger*," Pepper finked.

"Won't use the head on the *Plunger*? That's the funniest damn thing I've ever heard," Uncle Chet said.

Uncle Chet ushered me through the biggest house, in through the sliding glass at the back, through an airy living room with no TV, and out a wooden screen door to the driveway. I tried to look around because I knew I would have to give a full report to Flo.

"Let's take this one; it heats up fast," he said, pointing to one of the three American behemoths parked in the driveway. They had the license plates: PIPES 1, PIPES 2, and PIPES 3. The ancient blue station wagon, replete with wooden paneling, shone like it had just been waxed. We got in, and he flipped the visor down, and the keys fell into his lap.

"Are you still at the old Hart homestead?" he asked as we started out on Hazard Point Road.

"Yes, it's in the same place, but the old house is gone," I said.

My mother despised that little house. Letting her raze it was my father's last attempt to keep her in Keech. I don't remember much about it. I do remember it had a beehive oven and pumpkin pine floorboards, which, I guess, are special if you like old houses.

"That's a shame. I think that was the oldest house in Keech. I am sorry to hear it had to come down. Change comes whether we like it or not," he said, which sounded incredibly important and insightful. But that's because he had one of these deep voices that made everything sound that way.

But change didn't have to come to the little Hart house. My mother just didn't like it. In its place, she built a modern glass and cedar box that stuck out like a sore thumb. She found the plans in a magazine called *Rocky Mountain Vacation Homes*. It was on the cover. She had the issue framed, and it still hung in the front entry. Come to think of it, maybe we should take that down some day.

When the new house was finally finished, she found out that it wasn't the house she hated; it was Keech. Or maybe it was us. So she took off. And then Grandma died, and Dad and I were left with a house that was way too big for just two of us—four bedrooms, eight rooms in all. Our "great room" had a fieldstone fireplace and distant ocean views. It was the fanciest house in Keech Town. But it wasn't nearly like anything on the Toohey scale. Especially since it was our only house. And the Tooheys had a whole other neighborhood of mansions down by the toilet factory.

When we came down the driveway, Flo was up on a ladder, washing the big picture windows in the front. Dad would freak if he knew she was up there all alone with no one to hold the ladder. But Flo had a fixation on keeping those windows clean, like all of Keech would judge *her* if *our* windows were dirty. That ladder came out as soon as she saw a bird thinking about pooping. She turned to see who was coming down the drive, and I saw her expression cloud over when she read the telltale license plate.

She got down from the ladder, came down all the steps from the front deck, and approached us at the bottom of the driveway.

I didn't know what to introduce her as, so I didn't say anything. I didn't want to say "housekeeper." Turns out they already knew each other, greeting each other with curt grunts.

Uncle Chet explained what happened as Flo's reaction turned from mild annoyance at the sight of him to near panic when she realized I was wearing someone else's clothes and carrying mine in a plastic bag that had once held hamburger buns. She escorted me to the house, walking away while Uncle Chet was still talking. She pushed me up the stairs and straight into bed even though I felt fine.

After a whispered phone call, Ebbie arrived on her scooter with a pot of soup secured to its milk-crate basket with duct tape and bungee cords. Flo pinned me under layers of blankets. Ebbie came upstairs with a bowl of hot soup, took my temperature, and held my hand.

"She's perfectly fine, Flo," Ebbie said. I started to get up.

"Stay put," Flo ordered. I lay back down. I watched them say goodbye in the hallway. They had been together since before I was born.

I hope I find something that lasts like that, I thought, then I slept until Dad got home and woke me up.

"You went sailing on the *Plunger*? Are you pulling my leg?" he asked. He sat on the side of my bed, eating Chinese food leftovers.

"She nearly got killed on the *Plunger*!" Flo said. I tried to answer but sneezed three times instead.

"See that!" Flo clearly loved this evidence. "Now she's sick. You are lucky you didn't get hypo-pneumonia," Flo said, having a hard time deciding which disease the Tooheys had tried to kill me with. She gathered my dirty dishes and went downstairs.

I told my dad the story, and of course, he was thrilled. But I left out certain details, like the beer and the smell of booze on Uncle Chet.

"Chet and the older Pike and I spent a summer as pickers out on the blueberry barrens," Dad said.

It was like a bedtime story. I wished he had begun it with "Once upon a time on the blueberry barrens." I had heard these stories dozens, maybe hundreds of times. I had heard them so often I could tell them—all the versions of them. Sometimes it felt like he was just talking about one long summer day, and sometimes, it sounded like they picked blueberries for months and months, year after year.

There was the time they surprised a sleeping bear. There was the time some old movie star stopped and asked for directions. And now that I knew some of the players, I wanted to hear them all again.

"It was a great way to earn a few bucks in summer. Sometimes we'd get a ride. Sometimes we'd hitchhike. Don't you ever do that now; it was a different day and age then. Half the time, we knew everyone on the road, at least on the road out of Keech.

"It was hard work, but we had fun. We raked the low bush plants for those tiny little berries. You got sick of eating them pretty fast. And you complain about folding T-shirts. Try picking blueberries all day up in the hot sun. That's one thing about those Tooheys. Those kids were never afraid of hard work." He paused because I interrupted him.

"Yeah, Dad, that reminds me, Chet said your generation worked hard so our generation wouldn't have to." I immediately regretted it.

"See! That's why I gave you the summer off! It's all come full circle. Now Chet and Old Pike would be grandsons to Old Joe, the first Toohey. Not the first Toohey ever. They were probably in Ireland for generations, but you know what I mean. He had a good job—a good job for an illiterate Irish immigrant back in those days, that is—digging ditches. One day, he was digging some kind of ditch near a millowner's house, and he really had to take a crap. A big crap!"

"Gross! Dad!" I said, but he had surprised me with this. This was a new story.

"Well, it's critical to the story. If it was a regular one, he would have just gone in the woods. So he went up to the big house and asked, bold as brass, if maybe they had an outhouse. The millowner was out, but there was a parlor maid from Ireland who must have felt sorry for him or maybe she liked the look of him or something. Anyway, she let this dirty ditchdigger right into the front door of the fancy house and sent him up the front stairs to let him use the fancy bathroom. I don't know why she did that, but that's probably a whole other story.

"Now, Old Joe had never used an inside bathroom before. Like a lot of people in those days, his family had an outhouse. And bath time was a big bucket in front of the stove on a Saturday night. And sitting there, on a flush toilet with a view of the beautiful porcelain claw-foot tub, a shelf of perfumed soaps, and a basket of soft paper for him to wipe his ass on . . . mind you, people used to use the Sears catalog or even corncobs, which I don't imagine are very comfortable—"

"Dad! Again, gross!"

"Anyway, he had an epiphany sitting there—the epiphany that started it all. What the Tooheys like to call a 'come-to-John' moment.

"He saw a day when every home—not just new ones, not just the fancy ones—would have an indoor bathroom. Row after row of houses, tenements, apartments—all with toilets, sinks, and bathtubs on the inside. It was like he was floating up above New England, and he could see into every home, every millhouse, every tenement, and every farm. Toilets flushing and filling, water swirling, sinking, then rising again. Sinks running. Baths filling. Showers cascading. Shining porcelain; gleaming, curving pipes. He decided right then and there that he was the one who was going to make all those fixtures. That his fortune, his future, was toilets."

"Dad! Are you making this up?"

"Of course not. You already know how the story ends. I am just filling in the details. So he quits that ditchdigging job right then and there. His parents thought he was crazy. They were the last of the 'Old Tooheys.' Quit a good job like that! But he had grand vision, or a vision, anyway.

"He started smuggling booze into Keech Harbor with Freddie Alden, the black sheep of the Alden family.

"Maine had been dry long before Prohibition, and smuggling was everywhere around here. Smuggling's like a birthright to some people around here—"

"Our family?"

"No, we just counted it for other people," Dad joked, and we had a good laugh. And then he continued.

"At first, it was just booze from ships waiting a few miles offshore. Freddie had a fast little boat, and they raced out to the ships in that. They kept it and the booze hidden out on Alden

Island—and they would row it in later. That's how they never got caught. Old Joe had massively powerful arms from digging all those ditches. Old Joe could row a boat like Paul Bunyan."

"Paul Bunyan was a lumberjack, Dad."

"Well, yes, and I am sure if Paul Bunyan had to row a boat, he would have been very good at that, too . . . well, like some guy in a folktale anyway. Like in that Jeanette Frisé folk song. I almost met her once. I saw her in a coffee shop in Montreal, but I was too shy to say hello. She looked just like she did on her album cover."

"Dad! Old Joe," I reminded him. Can't have him going off on a Jeanette Frisé tangent.

"Oh where was I? Rum-runnin'—" *Ugh*! I hated when he dropped a final "g."

"Freddie. Oh yes. He knew Keech because the Aldens had the Big House here, and it was empty most of the year."

I knew all about the Aldens. They built the first house on Hazard Point—the mansion that Grannie Toohey lived in now, the one everyone calls the Big House. The Aldens were really old money—like whaling money or the China trade or something like that. The Tooheys married into the Aldens, and slowly, the Aldens disappeared, overtaken by the bigger tribe, until the only things left were Alden Island and a dirt road called Alden Road, which was abandoned by the town and eventually became a footpath. Nobody but old townies like Flo remembered that it once was a real road that had a name.

"Then, boom!" Dad went on. "Prohibition passes, and now there's more money than ever in smuggling, and they already have a system in place. They get their hands on a schooner; they start making the run up to St. Pierre on their own."

"Who is St. Pierre?"

"St. Pierre is an island. A French island."

"They sailed all the way to France?"

"No, St. Pierre's a tiny island off the coast of Canada that France kept its claws on, and it was like Booze 'R' Us during Prohibition."

"Near Campobello?"

"What? No. Off Newfoundland. Did you flunk geography, Valedictorian?"

"They didn't teach it."

"Where's your atlas?"

"Never mind the island. The story, Dad!"

"So they ran the stuff right down to Alden Island, then moved it right up into the basement of the Big House. The story goes that there was a tunnel—maybe it's still there. I wouldn't want something like that under my house. It would give me nightmares. I would keep thinking one of Flo's imaginary monsters sneaking in—"

"Dad! The story!"

"Then, one day, Old Joe moved back down the coast and opened a small plumbing supply store. Just before the Feds swept in and arrested a whole bunch of rum-runners."

"And what happened to Freddie?"

"He married Mary Toohey, Old Joe's sister. That's how come he's the black sheep."

"It wasn't the smuggling?"

"Please. Smuggling. Importing. Exporting. Who knows what the Aldens got up to, the triangle trade?"

"Dad! The Aldens were abolitionists! Maybe they used that tunnel in the Underground Railroad!"

"That would be nice, but it was marrying Catholic Mary Toohey that put Freddie in the doghouse . . . but I digress. The Tooheys started manufacturing plumbing supplies shortly after that. When we got into World War II, they got government contracts that put their toilets in military bases all up and down the east coast. So boom! The Tooheys made a fortune during the war.

"They are the best, you know. You can flush anything down a Toohey. It can take a whole cloth diaper." He paused while he scraped the last of the beef and broccoli in special sauce from the paper carton, first with a fork, then with his finger.

"Of course, when all those GIs came home after the war, they all wanted Toohey toilets in their new homes. Do you want any of this fried rice?" he asked, picking up another carton. I shook my head, and Dad started in on the rice.

"And now, they are the number one toilet in offices in the US of A because of the patented Silent Tinkle bowl design."

"Dad! Are they paying you to say this stuff?"

"If only! I'd gladly take a nickel every time someone's grateful for the Silent Tinkle. You've never lived in a house without a Toohey toilet. You have no idea how loud it is to pee in a toilet without the Silent Tinkle. And then there's their patented Flus*SSH!*—it's so quiet when you—"

"I get it, Dad; now every time I pee quietly, I will thank the Tooheys. I will be sure to mention it next time I run into them."

"Maybe you'll get to go to the compound!"

"I was there today."

"Holy smokes!" he said and spit fried rice on the floor. "Shoot, Flo's gonna kill me," he said, wiping it up with a napkin, trying but failing to get every grain of greasy rice off my pink carpet.

"Who knows what tomorrow will bring! You have a good excuse to go back. You'll have to return those clothes."

I had forgotten I was still wearing somebody's sweats. But they had already told me just to keep them. There would be no going back.

"Dad, really. I just want to stay home and get some organizing done." But the truth was I was afraid to go down to the village. I didn't want to deal with the disappointment of there not being a next time. I didn't want to sit there alone on a bench or the beach or at the library while the Tooheys whooped it up and my classmates all looked on. What would have been mildly boring would now be unbearable.

My summer had peaked. And it had barely started. And now, I didn't even want a job because that might mean waiting on the Tooheys, and that would be just too humiliating at this point.

The next morning, I pulled everything out of my closet to organize it by garment type and then by color—ROY G. BIV. But once I got it all out, I didn't feel like putting it all back in. I wondered what the Tooheys were up to today. Instead, I crawled in among the piles of clothes on my bed and took a nap; I didn't wake up until I heard Flo come in the house around lunch.

I know it sounds a little "Toohey" to have a housekeeper, but she was more of a necessity when I was little. After Mom left and Grandma died, Flo really kept things going, watching me after school and cooking dinners for us, too. Before I was old enough for sleepaway camp, it was Flo who drove me to and from all those enrichment day camps. I never even asked what she did while I was there. Did she go all the way home? Sit in the car and read? Run errands? All I knew was she was never late to get me.

"Hi sunshine!" she called up to me. "I brought in the mail."

"Okay."

"There's something for you."

"Okay."

"It looks . . . interesting."

Interesting to her, that's what she meant.

I just lay there, knowing she'd eventually bring it upstairs to me out of curiosity.

"What's this project?" she said. "Are we organizing by color again?" She handed me the mail and started collecting red items and putting them in the left side of my closet.

Folded amid the *Keech Town Crier* was a flyer from a Boston dress shop addressed to my mother, a messy pile of coupons, and an envelope of fine stationery—the aforementioned interesting item. I looked at it last to prolong her torture. It was addressed to me and engraved with the return address of *Toohey, Hazard Point, Keech Harbor, Maine.*

CHAPTER SIX

I opened it slowly, ripping the beautiful envelope apart and tearing its plaid lining.

"This envelope is wearing underwear," I blurted out.

"It's lined. I haven't seen lined stationery since my mother worked for the Aldens," Flo said, holding my only orange item of clothing. She turned and hung it between my red shirt and my yellow sundress.

Inside, I found a personalized notecard of creamy white, embossed at the top with a navy blue *T* that was shaped like a copper pipe. It read:

MY DEAR "FLIPPER,"

I CAN'T THANK YOU ENOUGH FOR SAVING MY SAILOR MOON, THE WORLD'S ONLY SCHIPPERKE THAT CAN'T SWIM. AND THE ONE AND ONLY SCHIPPERKE THAT'S THE LOVE OF MY LIFE. I HOPE YOU CAN JOIN US THIS SATURDAY FOR OUR FIRST OF SUMMER CLAMBAKE. WE RING IN THE SUMMER

AT 4 P.M., BUT WE'LL BE HAVING FUN ALL DAY. SO COME
EARLY AND JOIN US FOR LAWN GAMES AND SAILING AND
WHATNOT AND, OF COURSE, A GREAT BIG FEED.
FONDLY, GINNIE "GRANNIE" TOOHEY

It was like finding Willy Wonka's golden ticket. I was about
to shut it when I realized that Flo wasn't finished reading it over
my shoulder.

"Are you done?" I asked.

"I wasn't reading it. None of my business," she lied and then
stayed silent for a whole minute as if to prove it.

"You got a nickname," Flo said.

"Yeah? Flipper? I don't really get it."

"There was a TV show about a dolphin named Flipper when
you were a tiny tyke. Flipper was like Lassie but in the water. You
don't remember?" And then she started singing the theme song
"Everyone loves the king of the sea . . ."

"Oh yes, I remember," I said to shut her up, even though I
didn't remember.

"Now, Ginnie, the Grannie, she's the queen bee of the whole
tribe. Calls all the shots for the whole family from her throne up
there in the Big House."

I waited. There had to be more. Next to Bigfoot, trash-talking
the Tooheys was Flo's favorite subject.

"None of them make a move that isn't directed by her. Nothing
happens up there that hasn't been carefully orchestrated by that
old broad up on high. Everything from what they eat to who
they screw."

"Flo!" I had never heard her talk like this! Maybe now that I was out of high school, I was an adult in her eyes. Maybe she was trying to scare me off the Tooheys.

"Be careful up there. It's a snake pit. Don't look at me like that. I'm not judging. Just telling it like it is," she said, folding her arms across her chest.

"You think I wouldn't like to have a throne up there on Hazard Point? Make no mistake about that. But as it is, it's my lot to clean 'em. And since the Tooheys haven't made a throne yet that cleans itself, you'll have to excuse me. I'll be having a 'come-to-John' moment of my very own; only mine will be with a toilet brush, and you can finish putting away everything to the right of yellow."

Flo left to clean the upstairs bathroom, and I started to think about my outfit for the clambake, using the dress shop flyer for inspiration. I did have a pink dress that was a little like the one on the cover, but it wasn't something I could sail in. And it was plain, not patterned with tropical fruit and happy monkeys.

What fun it was to plan an outfit! I never had time for this sort of thing during the school year. Maybe I could go to work with Dad tomorrow and get something new in town. If there was more time, maybe I could have gone to Boston, and Mom could have taken me someplace. I fished through the pile of clothes on my bed and found the pink dress. I didn't know why it was still on the bed; I should have filed this with the reds. I held it up against myself and looked in the mirror.

Flo always said I looked nice in pink, but I couldn't see it. I pulled my hair out of its ponytail, and it fell to just past my shoulders. It was a pretty blonde, but I never fussed with it, just pulled it back every day. Maybe I should get a headband to match the pink dress. What if I dug out that makeup I got for prom?

"Wear an old pair of cutoffs and a t-shirt. One from your school or somewhere you've been. Something that means something to you," Flo appeared suddenly in my doorway, with her bucket of cleaning supplies and words of wisdom.

"Gimme a break, Flo."

"Listen, sunshine. I may be an old townie, and okay, I know I am not what you would call, *a girly girl.* I don't claim to know anything about fashion. But I do know a thing or two about the Tooheys. They hate a poser, even though some would say they are posers themselves. They're new money, relatively speaking. But they like to look like old money. So everything is worn up, passed down, and used until it dies a natural death. Frugal, like old Yankees, which I can appreciate.

"Anybody can buy a Lilly Who-sitzer dress, but only you were class valedictorian for Keech Town High this year. The one and only." Flo placed her bucket on the floor and walked over to my bureau. She whipped out the Keech Town High T-shirt that she had folded and put away.

"Here, wear this and those dungaree cutoffs," she said.

Flo never gave me advice. Something told me she was right. Even if she did use words like "dungarees." And they weren't cutoffs. They were from a good department store in Boston, and they were already cut and raggedy like that when I got them.

And that's just what I was wearing when Dad dropped me off at the clambake. I was a little nervous walking down the long gravel driveway. Every crunchy footstep seemed to announce my arrival. Meredith had just gotten there, too. She had parked her little white BMW amid the fleet of dark blue, American-made

Toohey cars. And now she was trapped against her car by two energetic and confident German Shepherds.

I couldn't believe it, but she was wearing the same dress that was on the cover of the store flyer. I thought that image would make a great addition to the flyer—Meredith pinned to her car by those two dogs. She gave me the once-over and smiled.

"You made quite the effort today. Don't you know where you're going, you stupid townie hick? This is their Start of Summer party. You're at the Toohey compound, for chrissakes. You look like you're going to the . . . Salvation Army party," she said over the barking.

"Really, the Salvation Army party?" I said. I stopped walking, turned, and addressed her head-on. "What is that? It doesn't even make any sense. Furthermore, it's the First of Summer clambake, not the Start of Summer party. And another thing, Meredith, I can be a townie or a hick, but I can't be both. So next time, choose your insult more carefully." I turned and walked on before she could see how pleased I was with myself. Then, I stopped and looked at her over my shoulder.

"Oh, and Meredith," I whispered very low, "I've got a nickname."

I couldn't believe all of that came out of my mouth! I never had a comeback! I usually thought of them once I'd had a good cry in my room. The rare times I did, I never had the nerve to say anything back! And there I was, in the Toohey driveway, telling off this rich bitch. I couldn't stop smiling. In all fairness, she was far less intimidating when pinned against a car by those dogs.

But then I caught a glimpse of my ragamuffin reflection in the side mirror of a Toohey sedan and cursed Flo and her stupid advice. Why did I listen to her! There was no turning back now.

Dad was down the road already, and it would take me hours to walk home, change, and walk back—we lived four miles away. Miles are long when you have to walk them!

The dogs left her and bounded toward me. One sniffed me up and down while the other held a clipboard and checked off items. Not really, but it felt that way. Meredith moved sideways against her car, ever so slightly toward the house.

"Safe, Jack, safe, Jackie! Hey, Flip!" Pepper called out, and the dogs sat down, noses still pointed at me but tails now wagging in greeting. Pepper threw open the screen door and came over to me. She was wearing a threadbare oxford cloth shirt. One sleeve was rolled up, and the other hung below her hand, monogrammed with someone else's initials. She wore it over a navy blue *Ogunquit* T-shirt and a pair of cutoffs made from khakis. It never even occurred to me that you could make cutoffs from khakis, but I guess you can make cutoffs from anything.

The dogs left me and returned to Meredith, who was still inching along her car door toward the house, picking up a layer of road dirt as her backside wiped the Beamer clean.

"Nice doggies, nice doggies. Safe, Jack, safe, Jackie," she whispered, but they ignored her commands.

"Hi Meredith, hi Flip," Pike greeted us both and sent the dogs back into the house with a quick double whistle.

Meredith planted an obscene kiss on Pike.

"Gross," Pepper said and grabbed me by the hand, leading me out of the driveway, through the house. I looked around as fast as I could—I knew Dad and Flo would want details—but we went straight through and out the door on the other side and across the lawn into the sea of family milling about.

"So you're Flipper," a lanky old salt said to me. "I thought you were one of us at first with that head of blonde hair." He looked like someone had cast a come-to-life spell on one of the "Ol' Salt" saltshakers for sale at Ye Olde Gift Shoppe. He had white hair and a trim white beard, but he wasn't wearing a yellow oilskin raincoat like the saltshaker but a Toohey softball team T-shirt and madras plaid shorts.

"I used to pick blueberries with your dad," he said. It was Old Pike! I almost shouted it out loud! It was like meeting Anne of Green Gables or Humpty Dumpty in person. He was Pike and Pepper's dad and the current CEO of Toohey Industries, Inc.

"Grannie can't stop singing your praises," he said.

How odd, seeing that I hadn't even met her.

"She loves that stupid, fat dog," he said.

"Weird, huh?" Pepper added. "She used to breed German Shepherds. Unbelievable dogs. You know the one that dialed 911, the one that made the national news? Saved his owner's life? That was one of hers. She had a knack for breeding. Jack and Jackie are her masterpieces. I swear they can read. Probably smarter than Cheddar. Ha!"

"Is that our Flipper?" I heard a cry from the top of the hill. It was Grannie—at last! I didn't know why, but I expected her to be dressed in an Edwardian summer dress, with a great big portrait hat and a line of servants trailing behind her. But when I looked up in the direction of her voice, I saw her coming down the hill in a faded *Campobello* T-shirt and elastic waist denim shorts that came all the way down to her tanned and wrinkled knees. She nearly tripped over Sailor Moon several times as the dog ran around her legs. The Shepherds flanked her, like the Secret Service. One wore sunglasses, and the other had a walkie-talkie. Not really, but it felt that way. She hugged me with strong arms that told of years of sailing and her alleged daily swims in the cold water off her sandy beach. Jackie and Jack circled around us, occasionally whacking the back of my legs with their fluffy tails.

"So glad you could make it," she said, reaching down and lifting Sailor Moon into her arms. "Oh, girls, I think Pike's going to need a hand with that pit," she said.

"We're on it!" Pepper yelled. Again, she grabbed my hand and ran toward the edge of the yard, yanking me along with her. I felt like I was going to fall down but then found my footing as the green lawn sped beneath my feet. It ended at the steep path that zigzagged down to their sandy beach. It was at the far end of Hazard Point, just around the corner so not a speck of the village could be seen. From here, all you could see was the water and islands and pines. Along either side of the path, early wildflowers bloomed and swayed in the breeze, but it was mostly overrun with the fresh green leaves of beach roses and beach plums, just now bursting into bloom as if on Grannie's command for the First of Summer festivities.

We found Pike poking a fire in the pit for the clambake. The pit was neatly lined with smooth rocks. It was a work of art. Above the rocks, a wood fire blazed, heating them up. Not far away, Meredith stood there with her arms neatly folded, her hip jutted out just so, but the scowl on her face was clearly unrehearsed.

"Grannie sent us to help with the pit," Pepper announced. Meredith rolled her eyes.

"Great. We need seaweed. Just pile it up right over here on that tarp, if you don't mind," Pike said. The fire was dying down, and rocks in the pit were good and hot. I followed Pepper's lead and gathered it from the water by the armload, getting soaked. I was so glad I had listened to Flo and worn what I wore. I probably wouldn't tell her that for a few weeks, though.

"What's for dinner?" Meredith asked ridiculously.

"Clams. It's a clambake, Meredith!" Pepper dropped another armload of seaweed down onto the pile.

"Just clams?"

"No, not just clams," Pike answered.

"Whatever else Cheddar and Uncle Chet bring," Pepper said. "They should be back soon. One year, it was just octopus. Tentacles, tentacles, tentacles. I thought I'd die of boredom chopping up all those bloody tentacles." I noticed Pike shake his head. I tried really hard to not laugh.

"She's just joking, Mer," Pike said. "Excuse me a moment, I forgot the burlap. You coming?" he asked her.

"I'll just stay here for now," Meredith said, looking down at her manicured feet. Her pink toenails popped out the front of sandals festooned with lime green daisies. They matched her lime green Bermuda bag, which she had carried with her all the way down to the beach. Why, I didn't know. There was nothing to buy. And no one here needed to steal anything from her.

"I don't want to ruin my new sandals going up and down that hill."

"Suit yourself." Pike turned and walked up the path alone. Meredith pulled a small mirror from her bag and adjusted her hair and checked her lipstick. It had never occurred to me to ever bring a little mirror with me anywhere. I didn't think I even had one.

"I was joking, Mer. They'll bring back all kinds of things to eat. There will be quahogs, littlenecks, cherrystones . . . " Pepper practically sang. Meredith looked up at her.

"But aren't those all different kinds of clams?" she said. "Where are they going to get all those clams?"

That had to be the dumbest question I had ever heard. Pepper raised her arm and swept it in the direction of the water. "The sea, Meredith, the majestic Atlantic, here at our doorstep, will nourish us with its natural bounty, as it has nourished generations before us. Where do you think they are—Mulligan's Supermarket?" Pepper said.

"Oh. So there won't be any hamburgers or anything like that."

"They're not going to find a cow swimming out there, Mer," Pepper said, catching my eye quickly and mouthing *dumbass!*

"I know. I mean, they're going to have to find a lot. There's like a hundred people here," Meredith said.

"There's forty-three," Pepper said, adding "Einstein" in a whisper only I could hear. "But don't you worry, Cheddar can root out clams like you wouldn't believe. He's like a pig hunting down truffles. He puts his ear down to the sand, and it's like he can hear the clams talking to each other."

"What she means is that Cheddar is reliable," Pike said, coming back down the path with the burlap rolled under his arm. "He always finds a way to get the job done. Sometimes, when I think about running the company in the future, I feel comforted knowing Cheddar will be there, as my second-in-command."

I dropped a load of seaweed, and some of it splashed water on Pepper.

"Sorry," I said.

"No, you're not," she said, bending over and digging her hands into the mud and slamming it at my stomach.

I could hardly believe it, but I found myself scooping up a big wet handful and throwing it at her head. She screamed and returned the volley with two hands of seawater and mud, which she scooped up between her legs the way a little kid bowls, hitting me right under the chin.

"You two keep that mud out of my seaweed pile!" Pike shouted.

"Your seaweed pile?" We both said it at once, switching our aim from each other to him, taking steps in his direction, flinging mud at his head. He ducked, and the mud hit Meredith in the chest.

Meredith shrieked. "This had better come out!"

"It's just mud, Mer, of course it will come out," Pike called out after her as she ran up the hill. On top of the mud, it was the sight of all that car dirt smeared across her retreating butt that sent me into hysterics, falling down onto the sand and taking Pepper with me.

"You guys are terrible," he said to us, as if we did this to every girl he brought home to every clambake every summer.

"If you like her so much, why didn't you tell her there'd be salads and baked beans and all that other stuff?"

"Why didn't *you*?" He asked.

"I don't like her," Pepper said.

"My mind is on the pit. I can't concentrate on anything else. This is my first year as Bakemaster, and I am not going to screw it up," he said as the last of the wood broke down into ash.

"You should tell her not to dress up like that. She's always so afraid she'll get dirty."

"That's just her way, Pepper," Pike sighed.

"Then why don't you just run up the hill and hold her precious little hand?" Pepper teased.

The *putt-putt putt-putt-sputter* of a boat motor interrupted this sibling bickering. Uncle Chet and Cheddar pulled up toward the dock in a beat-up Boston Whaler named the *Ballcock*, which was painted on its side. I looked the word up later. A ballcock is the thing that floats in the tank of a toilet, not something dirty—well, not that kind of dirty anyway. The boat was laden with bushels of clams, fish, and lobster, laid out in wooden trays with screened bottoms that were stacked high in the little boat. Cheddar jumped out, secured the *Ballcock*, and helped his dad with the trays.

"Wow. Where'd you find all this?" I asked.

"Mulligan's. He always gets the best. Already clean and ready for the pit. You can't beat that. Just order in advance if you have a big crowd," Uncle Chet said. I looked over at Pepper to catch a tiny smile on her face.

We helped add the seaweed to the pit, and Cheddar and Pike laid the trays on.

"Wish we had corn," Cheddar said.

"You don't get corn in June. At least nothing worth eating," his dad said.

"I still wish we had it," Cheddar mumbled. Pike soaked the burlap in seawater and covered the last layer of seaweed, secured with a border of rocks that had not been perfect enough for the inside of the pit.

"Thanks, girls," Pike said, standing between us and putting his arms around both of us. "I couldn't have done it without you. But I better go find Meredith. Ched, watch the pit." Cheddar nodded.

"Let's get out of here," Pepper said, hopping onto the dock and into a small craft she called a Sunfish.

It looked like a glorified bathtub toy, and we didn't have any life jackets on. But that didn't stop her from taking us all the way out past the island we hiked on, practically out of the harbor and into the Gulf of Maine.

"I've never been to sailing camp," I said out loud.

"Huh?"

"My dad found all sorts of camps to send me to in August. Enrichment camps. Theater, art, nature, music, French, swimming, kayaking, all sorts of stuff . . . but I never did sailing. Isn't that funny?"

"What camps are you doing this August?" she asked.

"None. He told me to take the summer off. He insisted."

"Yay. Cool," she said. "I am here all summer. Most of the time anyway. Sometimes Pike, me, and Cheddar go home on Monday or Tuesday, but we're always back by Thursday. On some weekends, the Connecticut cousins come up. We get enough for a softball game then. And Pixie is always here, of course. She lives here year-round like Gran."

"Cool," was all I could think to say.

"Oh, look at the time," she said, holding her hand stacked against the horizon. "The sun is two hands over the steeple of St. Columba's," she said, pointing to the Catholic church.

It was the one Flo still called "the new church," even though it was built—thanks to the Tooheys—back in the sixties. It was just a summer chapel, and it was mostly Tooheys who went there. Or so I heard. I had never seen the inside of St. Columba's. We went to the First Congregational Church of Keech. FCCK for short. It only sounds bad if you aren't from Keech and aren't used to seeing abbreviations with awkward letter Ks. We stopped going there when I came home from Sunday school wearing a shirt that said FCCK Sunday School. As I said, my mother was not from Keech.

"We better go. You get us back."

"What? I can't."

"We don't say can't. We say can. As in, you know, The Can. You can do this, Flipper," she said.

I'm Flipper. I can do this, I thought to myself.

"I can do this," I said out loud, and Pepper nodded.

"Okay, this here is your tiller extension; hold onto that. That's how you steer the boat," she said. She pulled a line, and the sail puffed out. Then she handed the line to me.

"That's it, that's it. Gentle. Now to port. No, port! Port! PORT!" she screamed. "LEFT! That's it! Great job!" she said it like she meant it. Once I got over my fear of screwing up and looking like a fool, sailing felt easy for me, almost natural, for the most part. Except that we were headed out to sea instead of back to Hazard Point.

"We better boogie," she said, leaning across me and yanking the sail full. She deftly turned the little boat around, and it scooted across the water in the right direction. We pulled it up onto the beach, and then I followed Pepper back up the path to the main lawn.

"Ugh, I reek," she said, smelling her own armpit. "Did you bring a change?" I shook my head. "I'll get you something. There's a ton of sweats around. Keep you warm for the bonfire later tonight."

Pepper led me up to the Big House. We went in the back door to the kitchen and up a narrow spiral staircase to the second floor, where she opened a door into a quiet hallway.

"All us cousins share big dorm-style rooms in the attic, but I will put you in one of the good guest rooms, and you can shower in peace. We have to share two bathrooms up there. It's a total drag," she said as I followed her. "This one's usually free; it's over the kitchen so it gets picked last."

She opened the door without knocking and moved a handmade door hanger from the inside knob to the outside; DIBS was nicely handwritten in black marker on a little card that hung on red ribbon. I noticed a few doors down the hallway had these as well.

"There's soap, shampoo, towels in there," she said, pointing to the bathroom. "Anything you might need, just holler. I'll bring the clothes in and leave them on the bed. You should have plenty of privacy. No one should be up here now, and now you have dibs on this room, so it's yours to use," she said, shut the door, and left.

To my surprise, Meredith came out of that bathroom. Obviously, she didn't know about dibs. Her dress was clean, but very wet where the mud had been.

"Hi," I said. She said nothing and left. I went into the bathroom. The sink and counter were splattered with mud—she must have cleaned her dress. There were two granola bar wrappers in the trash and crumbs all over the floor. So that's what she ate. And I guessed this was where she ate it. The bathroom was brightly lit and, other than the messes she made, spotless.

I knew she wasn't supposed to be in that room. I didn't want to get blamed for the mess, and I didn't want to dirty up the plush guest towels cleaning her mud, so I used a whole roll of toilet paper to clean it up. Although I knew the Toohey toilet could handle it, I flushed frequently because I didn't want to find out if it couldn't.

Despite the age of the house, everything in the bathroom was brand new and gleaming. There was a soaking tub and a separate walk-in shower. It was like something you'd see in one of my mother's house magazines.

I opened the door to the shower and fiddled with the dial until I found a good temperature. The water pressure was fantastic and the showerhead huge, like standing in a rain shower. TOOHEY TEMPEST was embossed on the showerhead. I got in the shower and picked up the soap. It smelled wonderful—sort of lightly floral, sort of lightly woodsy. There was just the ghost of the indented letters where the name was, but I couldn't make out what it said.

It felt good to get all the mud and salt out of my hair. I showered for longer than was polite when you're a guest, but I couldn't help myself. That soap, that beautiful soap! I washed myself twice over with it until I absorbed that scent into my skin. Then I got out and wrapped up in the giant fluffy towel.

The window in the bathroom was high up on the wall; no one from the yard could possibly see in, but it let in a refreshing breeze. I stood on a stool and looked out the bathroom to the yard below. I could see Grannie and the aunts making up a table in the backyard from two sawhorses and a piece of plywood. With all the hands involved, it happened quickly; each aunt knew what to grab and where to place it. They had all done it dozens of times before. Soon, it was covered with an old flowered bedsheet and dotted with giant bowls—macaroni salad, potato salad, garden salad, that awful salad with the green beans and the fried onion, baked beans, biscuits, and chowder, all served in vats to feed the sprawling tribe.

Back in the guest room I found, as promised, some sweats, a T-shirt, and a hoodie, all three emblazoned with the name of Pike's prep school.

Was it fate or irony? I didn't know. I was supposed to go to that school. I got in—I even got a small scholarship. Then, at the last minute, Mom bailed. She decided she and the boyfriend or husband or whatever he was then were going to buy a condo, so there went her half of the tuition. That's why Dad always dropped a mint on summer camps. It was his way of making up for it.

The sweats were way too long, of course, but I cuffed them, and they were fine. I went downstairs and found Pepper and Pixie out on the lawn.

More cousins had arrived, and the place swarmed with Tooheys. Toohey toddlers buzzed around with fuzzy blond tufted heads, gripping their balsa wood airplanes for fear of a sea wind taking them. But the wind had been mild that day.

Pepper led me toward the flagpole where the clan was gathering. Set atop a big hunk of bedrock that jutted out like the prow of a ship, the flagpole shot up into the blue sky. A flag gently waved as if it didn't dare spoil the moment. A big brass bell was mounted on the pole about four feet from the ground.

Someone handed me a shot glass of smelly rum, and all the chatter fell silent.

Uncle Chet climbed onto the bedrock hunk, his khaki shorts dropping low in the back, disgracing the moment with a flash of his freckled ass cheeks. He wobbled for a moment, then stood tall and raised his shot glass and said:

> *Here's to all things that run*
> *Be it a toilet or rum.*
> *So pour me a jigger,*
> *Thanks to that old ditchdigger—*
> *We get more flush,*

Flush by flush, by gum!

"By gum!" they all shouted in response and threw back their shots. I drank the rum like everyone else. Uncle Chet jumped down, and then Pixie climbed the rock and rang the flagpole bell twice.

"To summer!" They all shouted.

"Yuck! I hate rum!" Pepper whispered, tossing hers discreetly into the beach roses. It was awful. I guessed I hated rum, too; I wish I had known I could have ditched mine.

"Well, it's officially summer now," she said. I looked around at the crowd of her relations.

Imagine having a family that big. What did Flo call them—a tribe. It must be a wonderful feeling being surrounded by your people like that. I had no idea. My dad was an only child, like me. I had no cousins on his side. I barely knew my mother's family. What was it like to go shopping and have a sister go get you another size or color while you're in the dressing room, or a cousin jump out of the car and hold a parking space for you in the city. Or to have brothers whose mere presence meant you were safe from teasing or bullying but in turn teased you on their own. It must feel so empowering in an ancient sort of way.

There were so many Tooheys I couldn't hope to keep all them straight, although I was introduced to everyone. I knew that Pepper and Pike were brother and sister. Cheddar and Pixie were their first cousins, but Cheddar and Pixie were not brother and sister.

Then there were the cousins I met at lunch—the Connecticut cousins and Massachusetts cousins—the ones that only came up a few weekends all summer. And there were other first cousins, but they were either a little older or a little younger and weren't part of our group. Then there were second cousins, and first cousins once removed (children of the older first cousins). I think that Meredith and I were the only non-Tooheys there, if you didn't count the people who had become Tooheys by marriage.

I thought about making a chart, but then I saw Meredith actually unfold one from the pocket of her dress: a little family tree I caught her consulting.

"Cheddar's setting up the picnic blanket out by the lighthouse for us," Pixie said. I looked toward the far side of the lawn, and there was Cheddar, unloading a cart by the chain-link fence that separated their property from that of the lighthouse, which stood aloof and alone on its mowed acres of grass. There, a blanket was already laid out, its corners weighted with rocks. He placed a couple of cinder blocks down and a board over it and then covered that with a tablecloth. He pulled more beach stones from his pockets and weighted the tablecloth.

Then, with great fanfare, the clams arrived. They were transported to the main table in the bed of a Radio Flyer wagon, pulled by Pike and surrounded by the littlest cousins, making a racket with kazoos and drums and marching in paper hats that they had made at the kids' crafts table.

Uncles and dads lifted the trays and poured the steaming shellfish out onto the waiting platters on the end of the table.

Pepper handed me a plate, and we fell in with the rest of the clan lining up for seafood. We filled our plates and then went over to the picnic spot Cheddar thoughtfully assembled. It wasn't until midway through dinner that I realized what a nice time I was having. As the shadows grew longer, the chill off the water became more pronounced, and we moved in closer together. Pretty soon, we were all huddled together, leaning across each other and eating off each other's plates.

I had actually forgotten they were the Tooheys. I started to think of them as friends. But as soon as that thought formed, it hit me. They weren't really my friends. This was just a thank you for saving that dog. And at the next party, it would be just Pepper and Meredith and Pixie and Pike and Cheddar, and they wouldn't even notice I wasn't there.

I tried to push the thought out of my mind and just enjoy myself. At least I was having a better time than Meredith, whose stomach growled audibly as she picked at a plate of green beans. She sat awkwardly, trying her best to sit on the blanket in that short dress without giving everyone a view of her underpants—did they have lime green daisies on them too or were they something trashy? Those granola bars had probably used up all her daily caloric allowance. And she was too embarrassed to excuse herself, despite the benefit of the Silent Tinkle in a house so vast its feature was unnecessary. I was very glad to be lounging in Pike's old gym clothes. I was comfortable and warm and had no problem laying back on the blanket and soaking in what was left of the sun.

"Can I get you some potato salad . . . mac and cheese . . . a roll?" Cheddar offered Meredith.

"No," Meredith replied after each suggestion.

"And you don't like the seafood—none of it?" Cheddar tried hard to understand this.

"So that's what you're going to eat then—just those beans?" Pepper said.

"Yes. I suppose that's what you could call me—Bean." Meredith looked around to see if there was a reaction.

Pepper rolled her eyes, and when she did, she caught sight of someone that sent her shrieking. "Uncle Finn!" she shouted. She leapt up and ran toward a man standing near the flagpole. I never heard of a Finn before. He had gray hair, but he seemed younger than my dad. Aside from Meredith, he was the only other person there nicely dressed. He had on the kind of expensive casual clothes that city people wear when they come up here for the weekend.

Pepper brought him back to our blanket, and he got even nicer-looking the closer he came. I think most old guys wearing safari jackets look like they're going to a costume party. But on Finn, it looked perfectly fine. And he actually had something in every single one of those pockets: hand-rolled cigarettes (which he used when he excused himself to smoke, walking out to the driveway so as not to poison us); his camera (or as it turned out, one of his cameras); a cute little tin full of delicious little mints from Holland (that he offered to all of us); business cards (he gave me one—he had a non-toilet job: photographer—I'd have to show Flo later), and a monogrammed note pad that hid a tiny silver pen within its pages.

Finn was Pepper and Pike's uncle on their mother's side. Flo told me later on he had been married to Pepper's father's late sister.

Or to use Flo's exact words: "Once upon a time, they met, he asked her, she said yes, they said 'I do,' and then she got cancer. The end." She also said that he was a trust-fund baby, like I should hold that against him. But it wasn't easy to resent him because he was just so nice.

Then Pepper said something I never expected to hear.

"Uncle Finn, this is my friend, Flipper." I held my hand out to meet him but held on tight to the moment—*my friend!*

"It's so nice to meet you. Claire, isn't it? I heard you're quite the hero around here, the celebrated dog rescuer," he said. Meredith groaned. Was it a stomach cramp, or was she jealous? I like to think it was both.

Cheddar left and returned with a plate for Finn.

"Thanks, Ched," he said. "Oh, wow, look at that. You remembered all of my favorites."

I could see why they adored him.

"Is Scout coming? Have you seen him?" Pepper asked.

Scout! Now, Scout I had heard of. Scout was a legend in Keech Harbor. He was Pepper's oldest brother. He was so handsome, he stopped traffic. It's true. Someone I knew had seen it happen—right on Water Street at the height of summer. Scout was every promise of Toohey genetic potential culminating in one masterpiece. He was a bit older than us, already through college and working somewhere in Washington, D.C.

"I had dinner with him last night in DC, and I am sorry to report that Scout's stuck there for work. He sends his regrets. He says he hopes to be here for the Fourth . . . Listen, are you kids going to the Admiral's Ball next weekend?"

His answer was met with groans and sighs, except for Meredith who looked like a herring gull the moment you decide not to finish your sandwich.

"Then I am going to have to ask you all a big favor. You see, I promised those old biddies over at the yacht club that I'd take pictures that night. They have their hearts set on getting a photo on the 'What's the Buzz' page of the *New England Bee*."

The *New England Bee*—that was a shiny magazine that came out every two months, full of ads for the fancy dress shops and the yuppie kitchen renovations that cost more than the average house in Keech (our part of Keech, that is), as well as wordy wedding announcements that said things "Jane Snottington, resplendent in a gown of ivory silk and Carrickmacross lace, wed Biff Pilgrim-Mayflower in the chapel of Stuckuppington's Academy where first they met." Flo likes to take a red pen and correct the grammar.

"Now, I do have connections over at the *Bee*," he continued. "But I can't ask them to print a photo of those old buzzards with gin blossoms wearing their plaid party pants. But if you were going to go, I could send in pictures of good-looking young people, all gussied up. The biddies at the *Bee* would be happy. The biddies at the yacht club would be happy. And the picture would look so winning, they'd probably slap you right on the cover. And me, I'll make it up to you. I promise," he said.

"What do you think? I'll go if you'll go," Pepper said. It took me a moment, but then I realized she was talking to me. I was so stunned, I stayed silent.

"Well, if Flipper goes, I'll go," Pixie added. "And you know I hate parties."

"Me, too," Cheddar said. "I'll go, I mean. I don't hate parties."

"Meredith, you like a reason to dress up, don't you?" Pike asked, and she nodded vigorously.

She probably already had her outfit picked out. It was probably hanging in her closet already with matching shoes and purse and a typewritten list of nautical phrases that she could introduce into casual conversation, like *ahoy, cabin boy, fetch me a grounder of grog before the dogwatch*.

"So it's up to Flipper, then? What do you say? Will you help me out?" Uncle Finn asked.

"Sure!" I said. God. What would I wear? At least I had a week to figure it out.

CHAPTER SEVEN

I thought about calling my mom. She'd know the perfect thing to wear to such an event and where to get it. Maybe we could go to a ritzy salon on Newbury Street in Boston for manicures and facials, and I could get my hair done, too. But then, she didn't even bother to call when she got the clipping from the *Keech Town Crier* of my valedictorian picture. So screw her. I asked Flo instead.

"A dress-up party? We better call Ebbie," Flo said. "She waits tables over at that yacht club sometimes."

Within minutes, we heard Ebbie's scooter buzz into the driveway.

"Up here!" Flo yelled when the front door opened.

"The Admiral's Ball! That's top notch. You've got to go into the big city for something like that," Ebbie said, striding into my room. "All the way to Bangor?!" Flo said.

"Bangor? You clueless old hick!" Ebbie said.

"Boston!" Flo said it like a swear word.

"Boston? She's not going to a coronation! Portland. A nice dress shop in Portland. But then again, you can't look like you're trying too hard. Like you buy a new dress, but you take an old purse, but you're just a kid so you wouldn't have an old purse . . . also, it depends on who you're going with."

"The Tooheys," Flo said, again like a swear word.

"Shoot. Where are your dresses?" Ebbie asked.

"That side of the closet," Flo pointed left. She had rearranged my closet again by type because I decided the color thing wasn't working.

Ebbie shut her eyes and reached in. She pulled out the blue linen one I wore to graduation.

"Wear this," she said with her eyes still shut.

"You don't even know what you're holding," I said.

"It doesn't matter. You need the confidence of a gal who doesn't care what she wears to the Admiral's Ball, or them Tooheys will eat you alive like a swarm of no-see-ums."

CHAPTER EIGHT

My sky-blue sandals got scuffed as I walked down the Toohey's long gravel driveway. The shoes were new, but my dress was the blue one from graduation. Flo had steered me right about the T-shirt for the clambake, and now I was trusting Ebbie's fashion advice. I was a little nervous, until Pepper yelled to me from an upstairs window.

"Come up here to Grannie's room! Help me find something to wear! Ah! I *hate* these things!"

Of course, I had no idea where Grannie's room was. Aside from the guest room I had showered in, I didn't know anything about the upstairs of that house.

I had only been up the back stairs, but I was pretty sure Grannie's room was somewhere near the front of the house. I let myself in the front door, calling "Hello?" but no one answered, so I started up the main staircase in the grand foyer. The banister was a beautifully ornate dark wood with not a speck of dust, not even in all its nooks and crannies. I wondered who cleaned it. Is that a weird thing to think of? I wondered if I knew the person.

On the wall along the stairs, graduating Tooheys toting mortarboards stared out from beautiful gilt frames. As the years progressed, the schools got more expensive, and the smiles got straighter. I was disappointed that the photos weren't labeled. But why would they be? This wasn't a museum, although it felt like it had been curated. I turned toward the east at the top of the stairs and followed the sounds of Pepper's complaints.

"Hello?" I called out again.

"We're in here," Grannie called back. I found her room and went in. She had an antique bed covered with a handmade cotton quilt. Sailor Moon was curled up in the middle of it. She raised her head in a greeting that let me know she recognized me but wasn't going to like me or show me any gratitude or affection. *Stupid thing; she'd be dead if it weren't for me.* The west wall was covered with dog ribbons and framed portraits of smiling German Shepherds. There was a large window and a door, leading to a porch that faced the water.

By the window was a wicker chair and small table. A cashmere throw was draped across the chair, and rosary beads rested on the little table beside it. This must be the throne Flo liked to talk about. And Grannie sat in it, directing her prayers down the coast toward the toilet factory and beyond.

Voices seemed to be coming from the closet, so I entered. At the end of the wide walk in, a set of three steps led up to the attic door, which was open.

Warm, cedar-scented air hit me as I climbed the stairs and looked around. The stairs led into a cedar room that was walled off from the rest of the massive attic. Garment bags stuffed with clothes jammed rolling racks. Steamer trunks lined up against the wall. It was like an attic out of a story book, but everything was so beautifully organized and neat.

"Oh, I do love an organized closet!" I blurted out. How dumb did that sound?

"I used to have them arranged by decade, but now, they are organized by size. What good is it to look in the 1950s if you are a size 16 today? Good lord, I don't think I know anyone who was a size 16 in the 1950s. Also, they are not organized by the size on the tag but by the size they actually are. So a size 8 in 1962 might be today's size 4. That was a chore that took way too much math for my taste, but I am so glad I did it," Grannie explained.

Pepper held out a 1950s style dress, complete with crinoline. It was white with a blue toile print of lighthouses. "How about this?" she asked.

"That's a day dress. That's a day dress, too," she said, looking at me and indicating my blue linen.

It was hot in the attic, and I could feel my face grow hotter.

"Hopeless, the pair of you," Grannie said, and I didn't feel so bad.

"Have a look around," she said to me. "See if anything strikes your fancy, and we'll get you two dressed up from our stash. Over the years, there's been so many events, and everything ended up here in the cedar closet, so now, we just shop the attic," Grannie said as she flicked through the garments quickly on the hangers in front of her.

I moved toward a rack.

"Not that one, dear, those are all *plus* sizes." She made *plus* sound like a dirty word.

"Cheddar's mom," Pepper whispered. Odd, I hadn't even thought about Cheddar having a mom. There was no Aunt Velveeta paired with Uncle Chet. And I hadn't noticed anyone big enough to wear any of those caftans at the clambake.

I stared at the racks of clothes. The older dresses were carefully preserved in their own little bags, but as the dates got more recent, more and more dresses were stuffed into the bags. Grannie moved to another rack and flitted through the garment bags quickly. The metal hooks make scraping sounds on the bar as the dresses swept by.

"This," she said, holding out a blue dress embroidered with white flowers.

"It's like Sabrina's!" I gushed, like a starstruck fan. "I mean, it looks just like that black and white Givenchy gown that Audrey Hepburn wore in *Sabrina* but reverse and in blue." Another idiotic observation. Let them know I have nothing better to do than watch old movies every weekend.

"An Audrey fan. I knew you were a girl after my own heart. This cornflower blue is so flattering; it'll bring out your eyes," Grannie said as she held the dress up to me and gazed with admiration.

It was something I always imagined doing with my own mother in a pretty boutique in Boston or even just at the Bangor Mall. I couldn't believe I was going to wear that magnificent dress!

"Now let's find something for you, Pepper." Pepper took a larger size; I never even realized we were differently shaped until I saw Grannie looking two racks away from where she found mine. I was a stick. Pepper had broad muscular shoulders that presented a challenge for some of the vintage styles. Grannie finally found her a strapless fit-and-flare dress in emerald green. The color looked amazing on her. Once we found beaded evening bags, we left the attic.

Grannie did our hair in front of the big mirror on her antique vanity. She gave us both French twists. I loved the way her hand felt against my head as she smoothed the blonde coil of my updo. No one had combed or brushed my hair for me since I was little, and then it was Flo organizing my long hair into two neat braids every day, until I insisted that she stop when I entered high school. Can you imagine showing up to high school like that?

"Look at this, our own Grace Kelly and Doris Day," Grannie said.

"I don't want to be Doris Day. I want to be old, fat Elizabeth Taylor, I think she has more fun. Maybe I could wear one of those caftans instead?" Pepper asked.

"Don't be ridiculous," Grannie said.

"Can I wear the Alden emeralds?" Pepper asked.

"Not a chance," Grannie said, then turned to me. "Would you like to see them?" I nodded. I didn't even know what they were, but I pretended I did.

She opened a drawer in the vanity and took out a green velvet box. Inside rested a suite of jewels: emerald and diamond drop earrings and a necklace of five big green stones, each one framed in diamonds.

"Holy smokes," I said when I got a good look at the size of them—emeralds the size of peach pits.

"They'll be for whomever Pike marries someday," Grannie said. I wondered if Meredith knew about these Alden emeralds. Probably best if she didn't. And I felt bad for Pepper. Shouldn't they go to her? Stay with a girl in the family? Although some Alden girl probably cried when they were passed to a Toohey. *What would it feel like to wear them,* I wondered. Would wearing something magnificent make you feel any different about yourself?

"Have a good time tonight, girls." Grannie's voice broke my reverie.

"You're not coming?" I asked.

"No, I cherish these quiet summer nights when all the kids are out. Not that I don't love it when you're all here all summer, but I just got a new book from the library, and I can't wait to dig in," Grannie said.

"OK, Gran. Stay out of trouble." Grannie hugged us both, and we headed out, not for the driveway, but to the dock—we'd be sailing to the ball. I wondered if I'd finally get to meet Aunt Velveeta. I kept waiting for the right moment to pay for my ticket. Dad gave me cash. Finally, Pepper and I were alone, waiting down by the dock for Cheddar and Chet to pick us up in the *Plunger*.

"I have my ticket money," I said to her, holding out the folded twenties.

"Don't be ridiculous. I refuse to spend my allowance on this sort of thing. Why should you? The family always buys a mess of tickets; if we didn't go, they'd just go unused. Put that away." I heard some sharp complaining and looked up to see Meredith, clinging to Pike's arm, negotiating the dirt path. She was wearing a tight gown and shining metallic stiletto heels. Her gown was a gorgeous royal blue. One shoulder was bare, the other adorned with a big ruffle. The neckline shimmered with a tiny line of sequins that glinted and flickered in the early evening light. Her heel got stuck between the planks of the dock, and she took a tumble, landing on the dirty, guano-splattered wood with a thud. Pike helped her up.

"Goddamit," she said.

Pixie soon followed. She was wearing a pink dotted Swiss gown with a full ball skirt. "It's retro. Do you like it? Oh look, we're all retro! *Second-hand Rose, they call me second-hand Rose!*" she sang out.

"I'm not! This is brand new!" Meredith objected.

"Don't worry, Mer, we can tell you spent a fortune on your new dress," Pepper said.

"Check me out!" Pixie said, lifting the hem of her skirt to show she was wearing her red sneakers.

"Us, too!" Pepper said, showing off her yellow kicks. Grannie had told us to wear sneakers under our gowns. She said no one would be looking at our feet. I had Grannie's new tennis shoes on. She and I had the same narrow feet.

Uncle Chet and Cheddar arrived on the *Plunger*. The summer night was perfect with a soft breeze, no bugs, and the clear blue bay. Even Cheddar looked sort of handsome—stuffed as he was into that old tux. There was no sign of his mother. Maybe they were divorced. Poor Cheddar. He and Pike docked the boat, and they both helped Meredith on board.

Meredith's gown made her look like a million bucks, but it was so tight she had a hard time taking that big step from the dock onto the boat. Pike had to pick her up and hand her to Cheddar, who apologized profusely when he grabbed her boob by accident. Meredith swore and slapped his hands, which is a dumb thing to do when those hands are what's keeping you from dropping fancy-shoe-first into the ocean. But he didn't let go, and with a final shove from Pike, they got her on board.

Cheddar opened his arms and offered to catch the rest of us, but comfy in our sneakers, we hopped aboard with no problem.

Pixie, Pepper, and I went below to sit around the galley table so we wouldn't be too wind-tossed before we got there. It was Pepper's idea. She didn't want to ruin Uncle Finn's photos.

"Where's Pike? Where's Meredith?" she asked Cheddar when he finally joined us.

"They drove."

"What?!" she shouted at him like it was his fault.

"Yeah, she pitched a fit topside, so we hoisted her off the boat, and they're gonna take her Beamer."

"No fun!" Pixie scolded.

"No sense," Pepper said. And then to me, she explained. "It's just across the bay. We'll cruise there in under an hour. It will take them twice as long to drive all the way around the bay on those dinky back roads."

This put her in a funk for the rest of the cruise over. Having no siblings, I couldn't imagine what it would be like to go to a fancy ball with them or miss them when they weren't there. Although it did seem weird to be going there without Pike. I was used to the idea of them as a group.

I had never set foot in any yacht club, and I hoped it didn't show too much as we trailed Uncle Chet into the place.

"Make sure all the girls dance tonight, Ched," he said to his son.

I had no idea what the inside of such a place would look like. The rustic wood beams and paneling surprised me. Portraits of former "admirals" decked the walls. One stocky white guy after another; the only difference was the quality of the photographs and the eyeglasses. Those changed with the times. But not the navy blazers or the white captain hats with gold braids that looked like theater props.

Pike and Meredith got there only about a half hour after we did, so they must have been driving at warp speed. I felt a smidge sorry for Meredith, even though I know she hated me, because people made such a fuss over Pepper and Pixie and me in our vintage gowns. And I could tell she just lived for this kind of thing.

Meredith was acting the role of socialite, saying hello to everyone as if they were old friends. I actually did have some old friends there; two girls from school were waiting tables. And the guy who was tending bar had graduated a few years ahead of me. They seemed to have forgotten my name. Maybe they never even knew it.

"There you are!" Uncle Finn shouted, causing heads to turn in our direction. "Wait a mo'! I love this whole retro thing you have going on." He ushered us out to the deck and arranged us against a railing with a lighthouse in the background. Me, Pepper, and Pixie in the center, flanked by Pike and Cheddar, with Meredith next to Pike on the very end. He took a series of photos, and as we went back inside the band started up—a bunch of old fogeys in worn tuxedos. They played a foxtrot.

"Shall we dance?" Pike asked Meredith.

"To this? No!"

"I foxtrot!" I blurted out. He extended his hand, and I took it, sharing a quick smile with Pepper. I said a silent *thank you* for ballroom dance camp.

The band played "Fly Me to the Moon" as Meredith flew out the door to pout on the deck. I hoped she didn't hear Pike and me laughing—it wasn't at her. It was because we both started chanting "slow, slow, quick, quick" to remember how to foxtrot. We fell into the rhythm of the dance, and Pike didn't go out to console her until after our song was over. Pixie quickly dragged him back inside for a swing dance; evidently, that was their thing.

I kept seeing a girl from high school swirling through the crowd, serving plates of hot hors d'oeuvres. She didn't think I was cool enough to be friends with at school, and evidently, she didn't think I was cool enough for a scallop wrapped in bacon either.

I know they served dinner, but I don't remember eating it. We barely sat down.

After dinner, the band switched to the kind of music Meredith wanted to dance to, but the Tooheys were now done with dancing and on to drinking.

I had many glasses of champagne but only a few cheese cubes and a handful of mini melba toasts. And as a result, the shrill chatter of the crowd and the noise of the band were getting to me. I sat down and was just about to rest my head on the table when I heard Pepper's voice.

"Let's get out of here," she said and I followed her onto the deck and down the dock and boarded the *Plunger*. We dropped below deck.

"I wish we hadn't missed dinner," Pepper said as she rummaged through the galley fridge. She found a few doggy bags from the Dock n' Dine and, smelling each one, plopped the remnants of a few compatible meals into a pan. We had a mix of crabmeat stuffing, baked potato, and vegetable medley. Then we played cards on the bed in the master cabin, but I don't remember who won or what we played.

CHAPTER NINE

J woke to a headache, a dry mouth, and the gross breath of someone who ate leftover seafood before bed and didn't brush. I opened my eyes just for a second, and it seemed like my room was rocking. I wondered, am *I going to puke, is this what a hangover feels like?* Then it hit me. I wasn't in my room. I was still on the *Plunger*.

"What time is it?!" I asked, panicked. Was it morning? Was it still night? Was Dad looking for me?

"Uh, dunno," Pepper mumbled, face down on a pillow next to me. I hadn't told Dad I was going to sleep over. I hadn't planned on it myself. My own dress was over at the Big House. I was still wearing the vintage dress, now a wrinkled mess. What would Grannie think of me now? I jumped out of bed, stepping on Cheddar, who was sleeping on the floor, sprawled out on an arrangement of deck cushions. His jacket, bow-tie, and cummerbund were scattered on the floor around him.

"Morning, Flip," was all he said, then he rolled over and went back to sleep.

I could just walk home. I could dry clean the dress and return it in a few days. Then I pictured myself doing the walk of shame through the village as my former classmates poured morning coffees and the good people of Keech piled into church. Maybe it was still early enough to avoid all that.

I rushed up to the deck. The sun was already high, but the morning air was cold. I had never woken up on the water before. I looked around. The deck was damp. Uncle Chet slept on a bench, a yellow slicker pulled over his head. It rose and fell with his snores. He was still wearing his tuxedo shirt but had otherwise changed into shorts and deck shoes.

We weren't at the yacht club or at the Tooheys' dock. We were moored offshore. I didn't recognize where I was, but the land always looks different from the water if you are not used to looking at it from that perspective.

And wow, did everything look different. There were pines and rocky islands and rocky coast, but they all seemed rearranged. I didn't recognize any buildings on the shore. Maybe I was still drunk. Not a sound came from town or from any of the other boats nearby. The only sounds were the calls of gulls, the lapping of waves, and the *flap, flap, flapping* of the flag on the end of a nearby dock.

The Canadian flag.

CHAPTER TEN

I ran back below. "Pep, Pep, wake up. We're in Canada, Pepper, wake up!" I could hear myself sounding panicky and shrill.

"What? What the hell?" Pepper leapt up and followed me on deck, where I pointed to the red and white flag—its giant maple leaf waving in greeting.

"God almighty, Uncle Chet, what the hell have you done now?" she said.

"How long have we been asleep? We've got to get the hell out of here wherever we are. I'll get Cheddar. See if anyone else is here. You wake up Uncle Chet; he likes you."

With that, she jumped down below and shouted for Cheddar to wake up. He was up in a flash with the binoculars, scanning the buildings on the shore. No Coast Guard or harbormaster around yet.

"Mr. Toohey," I whispered in a sing-song, nudging the giant of a man as his body ebbed and flowed with his snores. I moved the raincoat off his head.

"Mr. Toohey . . . Chet . . . Chet . . . Uncle Chet!" I spoke variations of his name louder and louder. He finally opened one eye and looked at me with one big blue eye. I didn't know why, but he kind of reminded me of a whale.

"Flipper. Flipper," he said, patting the side of my face. "You're a grand girl. A grand girl. A credit to your dad. God, I love ya," The great blue eye shut again, and the snoring resumed.

"He'll be out for hours," Pepper said with disgust.

"We're in New Brunswick," Cheddar said.

"No shit, Sherlock. I had a feeling it wasn't Vancouver."

"That means we've got to deal with Fundy tides. Looks pretty high now," Cheddar said. "Where's that whirlpool?"

"What whirlpool?" I gulped.

"Only the biggest one in the western hemisphere," Pepper chimed in. "Did you flunk geography, Valedictorian?" I didn't know if she was angry with me or just teasing. It was hard to tell with her.

"Anybody know the time?" she asked.

I picked up Uncle Chet's hand and read the watch on his wrist. "It's almost noon," I said.

"Our time. One in the afternoon Atlantic time," Cheddar said.

"How's the fuel?"

"Almost gone," Cheddar said.

"That was probably a blessing," Pepper said.

"A blessing?" I asked.

"Yeah. Who knows where we would have ended up if we had more fuel. He probably stopped here when he saw it was nearly gone. See if you can turn him over. Get under there, and see if his wallet's in his back pocket," Pepper said to me.

"Me?! I can't put my hand in his pocket!"

"Go on, he likes you," she said.

"You can't move him. I've tried. And ten to one he doesn't have any wallet or ID on him or anything. Everything goes on his tab. And he's got tabs almost everywhere, but definitely not here," Cheddar said.

"We'll have to sail out of here. Do you know how to sail?" Pepper asked me.

"You know I don't."

"Oh yeah. But you sailed that Sunfish; you did alright for your first time," she said.

"Which one is port again?" I asked her. She turned me toward the bow and wiggled my left hand with more patience than I figured I was entitled to after asking such a question. I grabbed a marker I found in the console and wrote a big *P* on the back of my left hand and a big *S* on the back of my right.

"Great. Just don't turn around, Einstein. You take the helm. Cheddar and I will crew. You just turn the way we say to, and if he ever gets up, he can take over."

My stomach lurched at the thought of piloting the *Plunger*. I may not know anything about sailing, but I knew that the Bay of Fundy was a peculiar place with strange tides. And that whirlpool—I did not want to be within fifty miles of that thing.

"What's this guy want?" Cheddar muttered. We all looked to see an official-looking boat carrying an official-looking man toward us.

"Hmm. I don't know. I think he's just some guy," Pepper said.

"No, he's somebody. Harbormaster or something. Maybe a Mountie," Cheddar said.

"I don't even have a driver's license!" I said, feeling the sweat suddenly burst from my underarms.

"That's the least of our worries. Uncle Chet's wanted in Canada."

"What?!"

"Totaled a car. It wasn't even his," Pepper said.

"It wasn't even him!" Cheddar shouted. I jumped. I had never heard him speak above his low-energy mumble.

"Yeah, stupid Scout. We were at a wedding in St. Andrews," Pepper muttered. "Scout was so bombed he got in the wrong car and drove it into a rock. Uncle Chet took the blame so Scout wouldn't lose the internship in the Senate."

"Gran was so pissed she tried to marry Scout off to some bow-wow in a bigwig family up here, but he wouldn't take the bait. And neither would they."

"Uncle Chet was supposed to go to court, but he decided it was best to blow it off. Seriously, Ched, throw that tarp over him," Pepper barked. "That harbormaster is coming straight for us!" Then, she called to this foreign authority with a big smile on her face.

"Hi!"

"You folks from the US?"

"Yeah. We got lost. We thought we were in Eastport," she lied. "We were just getting ready to head back. We're not coming ashore. Are we at high tide now?"

"Oh yes. You better take advantage of it. The water empties right out."

"What about the whirlpool?"

"The Old Sow—that's in the other direction. I thought you were headed back to the States?"

"Yes, of course. We just didn't want to run into it."

"Hmm. It's the largest whirlpool in the world. The Old Sow can suck a boat down like a toilet. Say, 'the *Plunger.*' That's an interesting name."

"We bought it from a family who makes plumbing supplies, pipes, toilets, that sort of thing. O'Toole, I think it was."

"I think you mean Toohey! Oh sure; we have a Toohey. Worth every penny. My folks installed that in '74 when they built the house, and my kids have flushed everything down from diapers to report cards. Still going strong. You say you bought this boat?"

"Our parents did. We had permission to sail up to Eastport. Oops."

"I didn't realize Eastport had a dress code," the man said.

"What? These old things? Thrift store finds. We've been wearing them as a college dare," Pepper said. I was amazed—and relieved—at the ease at which lies poured from her mouth.

Pepper smiled and nodded and, every once in a while, looked over at me and winked. And then I remembered I had cash.

"I have cash!" I shouted. The ticket money!

"You have cash? What for?" the man said.

"Fuel. We need to get fuel." Pepper said. The man pointed to a fuel station, and Uncle Chet snored loudly.

"What was that?!" the man said.

"Look, a walrus!" I shouted.

The harbormaster turned.

"No, m'dear. We don't have walruses here." Duh. I knew that.

"Probably a harp or harbor seal," he said.

"We should get fuel before we totally run out," Pepper said. The harbormaster waved us on, and Cheddar steered us over to the fuel station. We spent all the ticket money and started home.

The hum of the motor woke Uncle Chet. He stretched and stood up as we passed under the Passamaquoddy Bay Bridge, as if his internal compass indicated it was now safe for him to emerge. He pulled up his shorts, which were sagging halfway down his butt, and walked over to Cheddar, and they whispered a bit.

Uncle Chet wanted to stop in a port where he had an open bar tab. The place was closed, but Chet poked around until he found the owner doing paperwork in an office, and he agreed to open up and make us something to eat. We had to use a back door that was flanked by piles of empty booze crates and smelly old produce boxes.

As bright as the day was, stepping inside the bar was like stepping into the night. It was dark, cool, and smelled like old beer and mildew. We sat at the bar on twirly stools, and the owner put on the morning news. While the Tooheys all stared silently at it, I stole away and used the pay phone to call my dad.

"Uh, Dad."

"Good morning, my social butterfly! I didn't want to wake you, so I'm sorry I headed out without saying goodbye."

"I'm not home. I—I had a sleepover with Pepper," I said. Technically, it was sort of true. I couldn't tell him the whole truth just now. He'd worry too much. Someday, I'd tell him the grandest Toohey story of all time. Just not now. *Once upon a time, just north of the border, I woke up in Canada*, I would tell him someday. After college. Maybe when he was in a rest home.

"Of course, I should have thought of that," he said.

"We're going for a sail. I don't know what time we'll be back. It might be really late. I might be sleeping over again," I said, adding to my pile of almost-truths. It occurred to me that as a goody two-shoes with no social life for seventeen years, I had never had reason or cause to lie to my dad about anything. But standing in the office of a closed bar wearing a ball gown on a Sunday afternoon, it seemed like a good place to start, and I was surprised by how good I was at it.

"You're a big girl now. You'll be eighteen soon. I trust you to make your own decisions. This is just the kind of summer I wanted you to have. And with the Tooheys no less."

"Bye, Dad."

I felt terrible for lying. But I didn't want him to think ill of Uncle Chet. Or worry. Or spoil my fun.

CHAPTER ELEVEN

After breakfast — or whatever that meal counted as—
Uncle Chet perked up and took the helm. I didn't trust him, so
I stayed close by, sitting on the bench where he had slept and
watching the shoreline. What if he got drunk again? I didn't want
to wake up in the Azores. Not today anyway. Not that I could
even tell where we were. At least when you are driving down the
road, you see signs that tell you where you are and how many
miles to your next exit. Here, I had no clue. I figured as long as I
could still see the shore—and the shore stayed on the same side
of the boat—we had to be heading home.

I had grown so used to the familiar arc of Keech Harbor and
Hazard Point that I hardly noticed them anymore. But these coves
and headlands were all strangers to me. Their hills and curves were
exotic configurations of rock and pine and shoreline and utterly
new to me, although they really weren't very far from where I had
lived my whole life. My dad had been all over Down East Maine
blueberry picking when he was my age, but I was hardly ever out

of Keech—except for camps. I understood now why people came here on vacation. It was all incredibly beautiful.

Cheddar came and sat next to me. We sat in silence for a few moments.

"Are you going to be a CPA like your dad?" he asked.

"No. I'm going to study finance."

"Uh-huh."

"How about you? What's your major?"

"Undeclared, I guess. I dunno," he shrugged. "I'm going to work in the family biz so it doesn't really matter what I major in." He was back to his soft-spoken mumble, as if he didn't want to commit to anything he said.

"You could study anything?"

"Yeah. Rocks for jocks. Frigging basket weaving if I felt like it. Whatever. I dunno. Where will you work after college?"

"I don't know." I laughed when I said it. What a funny question. How would I know that?

"That's kinda cool, not knowing," he said, and it hit me that, of course, his life was already mapped out for him.

"Does it bother you, having to work at the company? I mean, what if you wanted to do something else?"

"I don't mind. I dunno. It's not like I have some burning desire to be a doctor or anything. I figure the company pays for stuff, sailing, fun, prep school, college. Then it will be my turn to pay it forward for the next generation. I want my kids to grow up sailing and going to private school—no offense, not that there's anything wrong with, you know, public school—"

"None taken. I was supposed to go to Pike's school. But things happened."

"Huh. That's where I went, too. Imagine that. I wonder if we would have been friends. You're way smarter than most of those girls I went to school with, by the way."

Pepper joined us, squeezing in. It was the best place to sit on the *Plunger*, as it got the least spray and wind. "This is going to take for-frigging-ever," she said.

"It's okay. At least it's a pretty day." I shrugged.

"Chet's making good time," Cheddar said about his dad, as if he weren't there, but he was just a few feet away at the helm. "He'll get us home. He's got a big meeting Tuesday."

"Tuesday!" I shouted.

"Yeah, I mean we'll probably get home late tonight, but I know for sure he's got to be in Boston Tuesday morning."

"How come it's going to take longer to get home than get there?" I asked.

"This is the ocean, not Route 95!" Pepper shouted at me. "Who knows what time he left. Who knows what the tides and currents were like last night. Who knows what time we got there and how long we drifted around the bay."

"Okay, Magellan, relax. We're on our way home now," Cheddar reassured her.

"Yeah, but while we're up here tooling around, Meredith is digging her claws into Pike," Pepper fumed.

"Give it up, Pep. People are gonna do what they wanna do," Cheddar said.

"People hardly ever get to do what they *wanna* do," she said, imitating his voice. "Oh look—shearwater!" Her mood changed instantly at the sight of the bird.

Cheddar ducked below deck and returned with binoculars, a guidebook, and a beat-up spiral notebook.

"Gannet!" I shouted, pointing starboard.

"How can you even tell? It just looks like a big gull," she said.

"Audubon camp, three years in a row. See the black tips on his wings?" I pointed out like a true dork. "Northern gannets are the largest seabirds in the North Atlantic—they are in the same family as the brown- and red-footed boobies." I couldn't seem to stop myself until I heard Ched snort.

"Yeah," he said, laughing and thumbing through the guide, "It says here they can have a wingspan over six feet!"

We took turns scanning, identifying, and jotting our bird observations in the notebook—species, date, location. We gave up when the herring gulls became so numerous that we didn't notice anything else.

"I'm bored!" Pepper said and slammed the notebook down. "You're pretty pink," she said, her tone changing when she noticed my sunburn.

"So are you."

Then we both looked at Cheddar.

"Holy crap, you're cooked, Ched!" Pepper said.

"You've gotta get out of the sun, Ched," I said.

We got up, took our stuff, and headed below deck. I paused at the top of the stairs.

"Don't worry, he'll get us home," Cheddar whispered to me.

"Play cards? Crazy Eights? Gin rummy?" Pepper asked. We sat on the bed where we had slept, and Cheddar disappeared into the bathroom.

"Use spray!" She shouted at him.

I won at rummy, but Pepper ruled Crazy Eights. Then I fell asleep.

Sometime late Sunday night, we motored into Hazard Point. I woke up on the *Plunger* again, this time alone. Pepper was back at the big house. I wandered up the hill and found her in the kitchen, eating oatmeal for dinner. She was annoyed to find that Pike and Meredith had taken off alone somewhere and demanded to be chauffeured around trying to find them, but Cheddar refused.

"We're all wiped, and I have to get Claire home," he said. I didn't ask, but I guess she didn't have a license either. She must have been tired because she didn't fight him on it. I followed Cheddar out to his dad's massive Suburban. Uncle Chet snored in the back seat while Ched drove me home.

I was exhausted and sunburnt. My French twist had fallen out slowly over the journey home, spilling bobby pins all over the boat, but the layers of hair spray stayed, and the constant wind sculpted my hair into a rigid nest. Flo insisted on helping me comb out the knots. I think she was hoping to get some details out along with my snarls, but I didn't say a word.

It was a quiet week. I didn't hear a peep from the Point at all. I ran into Pixie at the library, and she said the crew had gone home to their real houses for a few days. I thought she would maybe want to get together and do something, but she didn't offer.

But I did get a call. From Mom. I couldn't wait to tell her all about graduation, my summer, the Admiral's Ball, my scholarship, everything. Well, almost everything.

"Hey peanut! Imagine my surprise," she began, "when I look in the mailbox and there's my daughter on the cover of the *New England Bee*!"

"Mom, did you get the other clipping?"

"You were in the *Bee* twice?"

"No, the *Keech Town Crier*. My valedictorian picture. Didn't you get it?"

"Oh, yes, I got that too. I am very proud of you. Your stepfather and I are both very proud of you."

"I gave the valedictorian speech. I came in top in my class. Number one. I wish you had been there." I couldn't believe I blurted that out. It was true though. I had wished that.

"We couldn't get away from work," she said. "It was too close to the end of the fiscal year." Whatever that meant.

"You could have called."

"We sent a check . . . and I'm calling now!"

"All I did to get on the cover of the *Bee* was go to a party. In a borrowed dress." Another sore spot between us. In town, it was a big event to go prom shopping. She missed that, too. It's a day trip to a mall down the coast. Mine came from the Sears catalog. Meredith's mother probably went with her. Probably told her how great she looked in everything.

Silence, then:

"The doctor and I thought we'd come for a visit, and you could introduce me to your new friends."

That turd face. What a joke. His doctorate is in business administration, but she puts *Dr.* on everything. "Let's not and say we did," I told her. That was the Pepper-preferred put-down for shooting down ideas. I hung up the phone so hard it rang.

Dad brought the *Bee* home that evening. And there we were on the cover—well, most of us anyway. Poor Meredith had been cropped out. OLD SCHOOL SUMMER FUN IN MAINE, the headline announced.

"Look at that, a daughter of mine on the cover of the *Bee*," he said. I wondered how many copies he had bought and given out at the office.

Then, later that night, I got a call from Pepper.

"Ha! Did you see it? What a riot. Must have blown the head-band clear off Meredith's head when she saw that. Ha!"

"She was the only one not in vintage, so maybe that's why. But more likely, she was cropped out to fit the shape of the magazine cover," I said.

"But more likely . . . she's an ass. Wait till you hear what Uncle Finn has planned as a 'thank you.' Remember, he said he'd make it up to us."

Make it up to us? I felt like it was us who owed him a favor.

"He's taking us out on a research vessel. He's going to pho-tograph sharks! In a shark cage! And then he's taking us to his place in Nantucket!"

CHAPTER TWELVE

"*It sounds to me* like they got you working for free," Flo said as I packed my bag. Dad supervised my packing, too. He was starting to cool on the Tooheys, and it was pissing me off.

"You do know what chum is, don't you," he said. "It's not a nickname for one of the cousins."

"Yes, Dad, I know what chum is. We saw that PBS special on sharks, remember?"

"As long as you know what you are getting yourself into."

"Dad . . . Flo . . . Finn chartered a research vessel. He wants to practice for a shark dive he's doing this winter in some place in the South Pacific. He's bringing us along as volunteers. We have to do a lot of the grunt work. But I think it will be fun. We'll get to work alongside some of the top shark researchers in the world! Can you imagine? This is a great experience. I can put it on my resume."

"Yes, but that's not what investment bankers mean when they say swim with the sharks," Dad teased.

"Ha ha."

"Your friend Timmy would probably kill for an opportunity like that. And all you did was go to a party."

"You're the one who wanted me to have a 'fun summer,'" I said, adding air quotes.

"I was thinking that you'd go to a couple of clambakes, hang out at the beach, and maybe have a summer romance."

"Gross, Dad." Of course I wanted a romance. But Pike was taken. And I didn't want to talk to my dad about it, no matter who was involved.

"I didn't think you'd be shipping out with the merchant marine." He was back to joking about it, so he had finally come around.

"It's only four days, Dad."

"I hope you won't end up . . . needing a bigger boat!" I tuned him out before he started reciting lines from *Jaws*.

Despite its fresh coat of paint, the research boat clearly had a long previous life in commercial fisheries. The 53-foot trawler had been used to smuggle drugs, was confiscated by the coast guard, and had been reincarnated as the *Just Say Know*. I know this because I read the brochure.

Meredith took one look at the grubby, utilitarian vessel, turned around, and went back toward her car, pulling her pink three-piece matching luggage set behind her. I had everything I needed for the trip in an old duffle bag. I knew to do this, again, because I read the brochure. I also sent clothes for Nantucket ahead with the package that Grannie would be putting on the ferry. Uncle Finn's cleaning lady would pick it up, and our fresh clothes would be waiting there for us. I knew to do this because Pepper told me to. Didn't Pike tell Meredith?

"What's the matter, Mer?" Pepper called out after her. But Meredith kept walking, as fast as she could in high-heeled sandals and a short sundress.

"Crap. Now I have to go after her."

"I thought you'd be glad if she didn't go," I whispered.

"It's too easy. It will take more than a fast flush to get rid of her. She'll just jump on the ferry and meet up with us on Nantucket with a steamer trunk full of outfits. And who needs that?"

Pepper was wearing old gym shorts and a ratty T-shirt from Pike's college. She jumped up and off the *Just Say Know* and jogged down the dock to the parking lot, catching up with Meredith. Soon, they were walking back toward the dock. Pepper even helped carry one of Meredith's pink suitcases.

"We don't have room for all this—all you get is one duffle," the captain said, glaring at her behind the aviator sunglasses that were perched on his sunburnt nose. He stood on the boat's deck with his hands on his hips. He had long curly brown hair pulled back into a ponytail, and he wore a T-shirt from the Montreux Jazz Festival. He did seem like kind of an ass, even though I enjoyed watching him give Meredith a hard time.

"I don't have a duffle," she whined.

The captain rooted around in a cardboard box on deck and pulled out a yellow duffle bag. It had the name and logo of a men's cologne on it. He threw it to her. Or maybe he threw it at her.

"Free gift with purchase!" Pepper shouted. "You love 'gift with purchase,' Mer."

Right there on the dock in front of everybody and the gulls, Meredith had to unpack her bags and edit her stuff into the duffle.

I bent to help her, but she brushed my hand away with what felt like a slap.

Meredith brought three pairs of shoes, four short dresses, two frilly summer dresses, a bathing suit, a cover-up, a sun hat and five sets of bras and matching panties. Five bras! Five? Did she take *all* her bras? I hadn't even owned that many in the course of my whole entire life. Plus she had a tiny suitcase just for cosmetics.

Meredith moved the neatly folded stack of candy-colored dresses into the duffle bag.

"Are you really going to wear a dress to scoop chum, Meredith?" Pike whispered and then sighed.

"What's chum?" she said, looking up, nearly in tears. Pepper kneeled down and spoke to her quietly in the nicest tone I had ever heard her use to anyone, let alone Meredith.

"Do you see that white bucket over there? We are going to chop up some dead, sorta rotten fish and put it in that bucket there. Then, we are going to mix it up with some nice warm seawater until it's good and stinky and maybe a little bloody. Then, we are going to dip a big scoop into it and chuck it—"

Oddly enough, it was the word "chuck" that seemed to do it. Meredith, already on her knees, leaned over the side and puked into the water between the dock and the boat, splattering the remains of the diet shake and iced coffee she had for breakfast on the side of the *Just Say Know*.

"Dude, you said these kids would be no problem," Captain Ponytail said to Finn. Then, as if to challenge us, he looked at us and said, "Okay, you *other girls*, clean that up." I think he expected us to cry or puke, too. Ass. We found the cleaning supplies on our own, then washed and rinsed the vomit off the side as if it were our life's ambition.

Meredith packed the suitcases back up and walked down the dock alone. Two slams later—the car's trunk and driver's side door—the Beamer peeled out in the parking lot, seeming to vanish in a puff of sand and dust it kicked up.

"I told her it wasn't a cruise" was all Pike said about it. Then he moped around the rest of the morning. He perked up a little when we saw a seal. But it wasn't until the shark cage went into the water with his uncle and we all had jobs to do that he finally snapped out of it.

Pepper and I continued to scoop chum over the side, and the boys prepped another batch. Then we saw a fin. A small shark, Captain Ponytail said. It was hard to see anything below the water. Was Uncle Finn safe? What was he seeing down there?

Finally, the cage was lifted up and with it, Finn. He pulled his face mask and hood off.

"That was fabulous," he said.

"Did you see a great white?" Pike asked.

"No, not that lucky on my first try. But I got some good shots of a tiger shark and a dogfish. It's all dress rehearsal for my trip to Tonga. I just wanted to make sure I felt comfortable in the shark cage and practice with all my underwater equipment. And everything went perfectly. And I couldn't have done it without you kids."

But of course, he didn't need any of us at all. He could have gotten some undergrad to scoop chum for free. And like Dad said, Tim probably would have paid for the opportunity to be on a real research vessel. But Finn created this opportunity for us. He brought us along, so we could share in the adventure.

It was close to six in the evening when we got to Nantucket. One of Finn's friends met us at the dock with a vintage red pickup.

It wasn't until we were back among the well-dressed tourists that I realized how bad we smelled. We rode over to Finn's in the back of the truck. I had never been to Nantucket. I had only seen pictures of quaint buildings and deserted streets, so I was surprised at how many tourists thronged the streets and how slow we had to drive to avoid hitting any. I dozed off for a second and found my head leaning on Pike's shoulder when we pulled up to Finn's place on the east end of the island.

I couldn't wait to see what his house looked like. Poor Meredith was going to miss that. I imagined the servants would line up to greet us like they did in old movies.

Hardly.

Finn's house was gray-shingled, much like a house in the Toohey compound but smaller, and he had only three buildings, the main house, a guest cottage (which was currently rented to New Yorkers for a big wad a week), and a small boathouse perched on legs in Nantucket Harbor, accessed through a path between towering rambles of swaying beach roses. That was also rented out for an even bigger wad because it was right on the water.

Unlike the Toohey's house, Finn's house had been completely remodeled on the inside. It was open, airy, and modern. The front of the house was traditional, but the back had been rebuilt. It was practically a wall of glass with views of the salt pond and, from upstairs, of the ocean beyond. The windows were spotless, and I wondered who cleaned them.

The walls inside were a pure clean white. And there was not a fingerprint or smudge anywhere. I don't know why I noticed that. Every wall featured paintings, local themes, lighthouses, ships, seascapes. There was one that showed the scene out the window but in winter. It was gorgeous, precise, and photographic.

"I love this," I said.

"You do? I did it," Finn said. "All I can see are the mistakes in it."

"Really? I didn't know you were an artist, too," I gushed.

"No. Not me. I am just a barely passable photographer. I only did the one painting. I know it's vain to hang it here beside all the real art but it means a lot to me. I painted it one winter when I was here alone. It was a difficult time. One of my renters left the paints, brushes, and the big canvas in the garage. So I thought, why not?"

I wondered if that was when his wife died. When our neighbor's wife died, he went out and got remarried three months later. And here was Uncle Finn, sitting alone in Nantucket all winter just painting.

"And just like that, you painted a masterpiece," I said.

"A masterpiece," he laughed. "You're sweet, kid. It was a tough year. So I just focused on the painting. Do you like mornings?" he asked me, changing the subject.

"Yes?"

"Great. I've put you and Pep in one of the east bedrooms. You'll get a great sunrise and a wonderful breeze. Go on up, have a shower, *please,*" he joked a little, "rest, and come down and join us when you're ready. A few friends are going to stop by a little later. We'll eat around eight. Nothing fancy. Just stuff to nibble on."

"It's the third door on the top of the stairs to the left," he said.

I climbed the stairs, taking in the view through the wall of glass. I found our guest room. We had a king-sized canopy bed and a white wicker seating area. Pepper had already showered. She was wrapped in a white terry robe and tracking water all over the wood floor.

"I left the water on for you," she said, pointing to the bathroom. Steam billowed out of the door.

I stepped over Pepper's smelly clothes on the floor, added my own, and got in. I was never so happy to take a shower—finally getting the smell of fish out of my hair and skin. And that soap! It was geranium-scented and made in Sweden. I almost stole a bar. He'd never notice, but I liked Finn too much. I wrapped up in the other plush bathrobe and then flopped onto the bed.

The sun was setting when I woke up with my face in a puddle of drool. Laughter and chatter echoed up from downstairs. At first, I thought it was the TV. But then I remembered I hadn't even seen one. It must have been the "few friends" coming over in the evening. I put on those distressed jeans that Flo hates and a pink T-shirt. I tamed my hair into a ponytail and descended the stairs into a sea of pastel silks and linens. I was grossly underdressed.

Was this something Pepper was supposed to tell me about, I wondered. I wanted to just go back upstairs and hide, but it was too late.

"Another one awakens," a man said to me as I got to the bottom of the stairs. He wore a tan linen suit and no shoes. The woman he was with looked me up and down. She wore a sleeveless white silk dress. Her arms were skinny and toned, and she wore a massive gold cuff on each wrist. She sipped a glass of red wine. I watched her for a moment, waiting for her to dribble that wine on her white silk dress, but she didn't. I was uncomfortable around these fancy adults, and I was also scared of this lady who had the power to drink red wine while wearing white silk.

"A few friends" turned out to be around fifty. "Nothing fancy" turned out to be passed hors d'oeuvres and a full buffet. A uniformed caterer floated by with a tray of tiny architectural bits of puff pastry stuffed with a variety of fillings that I was too tired to identify.

Then, I heard a cackle—Pepper's unmistakable laugh—coming from the kitchen. I excused myself, curtsied for some unknown reason, and went down the hall. Pepper, Pike, and Cheddar sat around the island in the kitchen with the catering staff working around them. Like me, they were in jeans.

"It's about time, Sleeping Beauty. I thought we'd have to send Pike to kiss you awake," Pepper said. God, she could be mean when she wanted to. I prayed no one saw how red I got.

We stayed in the kitchen. The Tooheys thought nothing of grabbing food from the caterers' carefully arranged trays. The caterers didn't say a word but silently replenished them before they were delivered to the better-dressed guests.

Cheddar seemed content, but Pepper was twitchy, bored maybe. I know I was bored and cramped by the presence of the sophisticated guests, their quiet manners, and their delicate clothes.

"Let's pack it up and go hang out by the fire pit at the boathouse," Pike said, practicing his leadership skills.

"That's a great idea!" the caterer said, the first words I had heard her say to us since I came downstairs.

"I thought it was rented out," Cheddar said.

"So what? They won't care. They're probably not even there. I don't see any lights on," Pike said.

"Let me put something together for you!" the caterer said. She sounded overjoyed to get rid of us. She packed a little bit of everything into an aluminum pan, with a package of utensils and napkins.

"I will get some soda," Pepper announced loudly and mechanically.

Cheddar carried the pan outside and down the deck stairs to the backyard. Pepper quickly took the lead, guiding the way with the flashlight, and cradling the tote bag with the soda close to her chest like it was her precious baby.

"Ooh, shooting star!" Pike said as we got halfway across the yard, away from the lights of the house. We stopped to look, and then we lost Pepper and Cheddar somewhere in the darkness. They must have already gone down the path through the beach roses.

"Whoa, it's dark here," he said. And suddenly, his voice was the only sound that seemed to matter—even as the party noise tinkled behind us, the crickets chimed, the beach roses swished in the wind, and the water lapped somewhere unseen.

"At Hazard Point, we always have the lighthouse or the buoy lights. It's never dark like this," he said.

"Look at the Milky Way!" I said as our eyes adjusted to the darkness, the sky growing more amazing.

"Are we still in the yard? I can't tell." I stumbled along as we tried to find the path without Pepper's flashlight.

"We're where the beach roses start, but I can't find the path."

Then, with a *woosh*, something large ran in front of us—a deer, huge and swift, its pounding hoofbeats seemed to echo my own heartbeats and then take them over, replacing my rhythm with its own. Even though I've seen deer a million times before, this time, it was thrilling and scary to be so close to one at night, under the heavy banner of stars, in the potent perfume of the blooming beach roses that the deer had disturbed and sent wafting around us—and we grabbed each other in surprise.

"Oh, sorry. That buck surprised me," Pike said but didn't let me go.

I pretended to be a little more afraid than I was. It was lovely there, in Pike's arms in the darkness. Lovely sounds like a corny word, but that's what it was. The hoofbeats of that wild creature still echoing in my head, the rumble and scent of ocean and beach roses, the *boom* and *swish* of the waves in the distance, and Pike, tall and responsible, warm and strong, smelling so slightly of that geranium soap.

Then, *swish-swish-swish-swish* through the path came a flash of light, and suddenly, there was Cheddar. Pike's arms fell away. I took a step back and froze in the beam of light.

"Be careful of ticks," Cheddar announced, shining the flashlight in my face. "And the rocks. I'll light the way. Pepper shouldn't have run off so fast. It's hard enough to find the path in broad daylight," he said, turning and pointing the flashlight at the path.

Pepper had unpacked the food. The precious architectural appetizers looked out of place around the fire pit, like someone wearing street shoes at the beach. Or like Meredith on the dock. I hoped it didn't remind Pike of her. The pit was a fancy one, a neat circle of curved stones surrounded by a quartet of Adirondack chairs with matching cocktail tables.

"No scallops wrapped in bacon?" Cheddar asked.

"Nope! But there's green apple slices with blue cheese perched on a wonton," Pepper said.

"Good thing we ate on the boat," Pike said, as he popped two wontons into his mouth.

"Ta da!" Pepper said, after digging into her tote bag; she presented the "soda," which turned out to be beer bottles, one for each of us. I didn't know how she managed that. There were two bartenders.

I don't remember what we talked about around the fire. Was it the trip? The shark? The chum? Finn's house? The party? It was probably the general nonsense they often engaged in, like repeating the same joke over and over until everyone has said it at least once. I was too busy reliving the memory of being in Pike's arms. I felt sorry for Meredith and, in the same instant, was so glad she was gone.

Sometime around midnight, the people renting the boathouse came back from dinner. They could barely get their boat docked and nearly fell in the water disembarking, which they thought was hilarious, because they were totally bombed.

"We got the fire pit all ready for you," Pepper said.

"Great!" one of the men said, while his wife howled with laughter. The other couple stumbled down to the pit. The woman tried to sit on one of the Adirondack chairs around the pit but managed to miss it and landed on the sand, laughing and exposing her underpants to her friends, who laughed even harder.

"Joanie, it would be nice if one night ended without a view of your crotch," the other woman said, as she tripped over her friend and landed on the ground next to her.

Her husband didn't bother to help her up; instead, he wrapped a thick arm around me, pulling me against his fat gut.

"Look at this beauty. If I was only ten years younger—" he said.

I didn't have a chance to respond before Cheddar did.

"More like forty, you gross perv," Cheddar said loudly, wedging himself between us so the man had no choice but to drop his arm.

"Huh?" he said, seeming confused. I shuddered, and for a moment, it felt like his warm hairy arm was still there. I looked at Ched with relief.

I was glad when we left them at the fire pit, but I wondered if it was safe to leave drunks around so many hazards—fire, the dock, deep water. But we went back up to the house anyway.

The return trip was easier with the lights of the house guiding us.

I kept hoping that Pike would pull me aside and hold me again. But we all marched single file through the beach roses, through the yard and flower gardens that I could see now that my eyes had adjusted to the dark, and back up to the house.

With all those windows lit up from within, the back of the house looked like panels in a comic book: a party winding down in one panel, a handful of party guests clustered around Finn as he played the piano; in another panel, a guest reapplied lipstick; tired waitstaff cleaning up the kitchen. Upstairs was in darkness. No illicit romances here.

We entered through the kitchen. It was clean and deserted. A few nonperishable snacks and desserts were left out. The bartenders were gone, and what was left from the bar was lined up on the kitchen island—a few bottles of wine and an assortment of foreign beers.

"That lady looks just like Jeanette Frisé," I blurted out loud, starstruck, as I looked down the hallway into the great room.

"Who?" Pepper asked.

"That lady there. She looks like a folk singer from Quebec that my dad's nuts about."

The lady approached us.

"Her dad is nuts about you," Pepper said.

"He must be a very handsome man to have such a *belle fille*," she said with a hint of an accent. It was Jeanette Frisé. It was friggin' Jeanette Frisé.

"Jeanette," she said, holding out her hand.

"Claire," I said.

"*Enchanté,*" she replied. She refilled her wine glass and left. Later, I held her hair back when she vomited in the bathroom.

CHAPTER THIRTEEN

Uncle Finn was up early the next morning, making a breakfast feast for us.

First came the strawberry crepes with strawberries he picked from his own patch.

"Look at that, like a perfect little gemstone." He held up a berry for us to admire. "And sadly, they're the last of the season," he sighed and carefully cut it into thin slices. Thank God we didn't trample them in the night.

As we settled around the table, he made us café au lait with coffee made in a little pot he had picked up in France. He whipped up the foam in a little gadget he had brought home from Italy.

Then, he made us omelets with eggs from a family farm on the west side of the island and cheese and vegetables left over from the party the night before.

"The best part of any party is eating well for a week afterward with little effort," he said.

The cleaning lady came while we were eating. She was about twenty-two and from somewhere in Europe, but no one knew exactly where. She wore a low-cut tank top and bent at the waist to pick up everything on the floor. I was embarrassed for her, even though I knew she did it on purpose and wanted everyone to see everything.

"Geez, Uncle Finn," Pepper said. The boys snickered.

"I know. She is a good worker, though. And she's a good soul. Sends a lot of money home to her family. She just wants someone to notice her, that's all . . . " he said kindly, then changed to a serious tone and whispered, "When you have money, you're always a target. You should know that, kids. Just be aware of it."

"We know. Grannie drills us. But we aren't rich like you," Pepper said.

"What's rich? It's all relative. You kids that don't work all summer are rich to the kids that have to." I was surprised to hear myself included in any group described as "rich."

"But that guy over there," he said, pointing to a house whose chimneys were barely visible between the breaks in the tall vegetation, "I am an ant compared to him. They use that house for two weeks in July—only. The rest of the time, it sits empty. Empty. And staffed. They don't even rent it out. Let someone else get some enjoyment of the place. He doesn't need the money. Neither do I. But I like knowing my house isn't lonely and it's being enjoyed. I rent this place out all summer. Except for this one week when I have a party and see all my friends."

"Where do you live for the rest of the summer?" I asked.

"I travel. I go to Maine for the big First of Summer party, of course; I wouldn't miss that for the world. But then I take off again—I do my northern hemisphere trips, I leave for a tour of Mongolia by camel next month. I can't wait. I live here most of the winter, but travel all of February. I hate February. I go somewhere warm, like Tonga.

"But how rich am I really?" he went on. "I'll tell you. My one week in summer here and I have all of you here with me. Now that's truly rich," he said, lifting a glass of freshly squeezed grapefruit juice in a toast. If I didn't know his tragic past, I would think he might be full of crap.

Uncle Finn flew us home two days later in a plane he rented. He said owning your own plane is for the birds.

I thought that if I were a forty-year-old woman, I would be madly in love with Uncle Finn. I didn't blame his cleaning lady one bit, even though she looked like a complete skank and was going about it all wrong—not that I had much experience in that department.

Uncle Chet picked us up at a tiny airport I didn't even know existed. He came with Grannie in her ancient Ford wagon. Pepper flew into her grandmother's arms immediately. It was cute to see.

"Mission accomplished," she said to her grandmother, as Grannie wrapped her strong arms around her.

"Glad to hear it, Pep," she said and kissed the top of her head. "Glad to hear it."

Aw, that's cute, I foolishly thought.

All I could think of was what fun I was having.

To recap, I had:

- Been to the First of Summer cookout at the Tooheys'.
- Gone to the Admiral's Ball.
- Learned to sail.

- Been to Canada.
- Been on the cover of the *New England Bee.*
- Crewed on a research vessel in Nantucket Sound.
- Held Jeanette Frisé hair while she puked.

And it wasn't even July.

CHAPTER FOURTEEN

"*Now that you're one* of the gang, you're going to get a job to do like the rest of them. You're on chowder duty," Grannie said, welcoming me into the kitchen, as they prepped for their big Fourth of July party. She took out an apron with blueberry appliqués, slipped it over my head, and tied it behind my back.

Pepper sat before a huge mound of potatoes. We had to peel and chop every single one.

I sat down on one of the high stools at the worktable, picked up a peeler, and got to work.

"It's about time you showed up," Pepper said, as she picked up her cutting board and slid her potato chunks into the pot in the middle of the table.

Cheddar didn't even look up. His fingers deftly shucked one clam open after another, flinging their goopy bodies into a big metal bowl and tossing the shells into a bucket on the floor.

"I swear I can hear each one scream," Pixie said, cringing. She had been peeling the same patch on the same potato since I walked in. Tiny slivers of potato peel dropped like feathers into the bowl she worked over.

"You should have come on shark patrol with us," Pepper said.

"Ugh, no thank you," she said.

"You would have loved Nantucket, Pix," Pike said.

"Maybe so . . . And no fair you hogging Flipper all to yourselves, for a whole week practically."

"It's your own fault you didn't come," Pepper said.

"Well, dibs on Flipper for Wednesday," Pixie said.

"You can't call dibs on her; she's a person," Cheddar said.

"Maybe she doesn't want to hang around with you all day on Wednesday being bored out of her mind," Pepper said.

"Oh please, Flipper!" Pixie said.

"Sure," I said. I didn't want to be rude.

Pepper rolled her eyes and pushed another chopped potato into the pot. Once we were done with the potatoes, Pepper and I chopped the onions and celery. Pike was in charge of sautéing the onions and adding the ingredients. Pixie dropped her potato on the floor and then chucked it into the compost bucket.

"And now it's time for Grannie's secret ingredient," Pike said.

"What's that?" I asked.

"Grannie won't tell you until you marry Pike," Pepper said. This time, I knew they could see me blush. I hoped they'd chalk it up to the heat of the kitchen.

"Big secret; it's Bell's Seasoning. That's why it smells like Thanksgiving in here," Cheddar said.

"Spoilsport," Pepper said.

I had a giggle to myself because this was getting to be just like one of my enrichment camps but without getting a certificate or badge to prove I did it. Now, I could add Chowder Cooking to

Sailing and Shark Research and Stealth Alcohol Consumption. Imagine what those badges would look like. I could just imagine Grannie handing them out in a ceremony in late August. Maybe they did rum-running drills for an Alden Times badge.

With the chowder on the stove, Grannie assigned us all new jobs. Pixie had to watch the stove. Basically, she had to keep an eye on a giant stockpot set to low simmer to make sure it didn't boil dry. Sounded risky for her, just the same. Cheddar had to go rearrange the cars in the driveway to make room for more. Pike, Pepper, and I were assigned to get the chairs and tables from the basement.

"You guys go downstairs. I'll go open the bulkhead door from outside," Pepper said.

Pike opened the basement door and flicked on the light. I followed him down the stairs into the musty damp air. The folding chairs and tables were lined up by the wall. This party was for more than just family. It was for their friends and business associates and all sorts of toilet industry big shots. We needed more chairs and tables than for the last party. So, we had to use all of them, even the ones that hadn't been cleaned yet. They were shoved up against the back wall and covered with a thick layer of dust. Spiders scurried when I went to lift a chair. I swore I felt one crawl up my leg.

Pike was able to carry six chairs at a time, and I could manage only two. It seemed like it would have made more sense to send Cheddar down to do this. But I was grateful to be included, so I didn't complain. We carried them over to the bulkhead door. Pike put his stack down to open the door.

"I don't get it," Pike said, as he shook one of the doors. "This locks from the inside—and it's unlocked—but it feels like it's locked from the outside. Wasn't Pepper going to open it for us, anyway?" He said as he shook the doors, but they wouldn't open.

Just then, the lights went out.

"Put the lights back on!" he shouted. Something brushed against my leg. I screamed and dropped the chairs.

"What's the matter?" Pike said.

"There's something down here. Something moving around with fur."

"No, it's probably nothing. Just a piece of cobweb, maybe. There's a ton of spiders down here," he said.

"That's not any better." Now the spiders in my imagination became hairy and big. They joined the rats I couldn't help but picture. Rats sneaking in through Freddie Alden's secret rum-running tunnel. Rats wearing trench coats, waving their friends through to the basement. Spiders dropping down like animated stalactites. I thought I felt it again. This time, I jumped and tripped over the chairs I dropped.

"Where are you?" Pike said.

"Here," I said, reaching out in the darkness.

Pike carefully made his way toward me over the chairs I dropped. I felt his hand brush my shoulder, feel along my elbow, and finally grasp my hand. He pulled me up to his side, wrapping an arm around me.

"It's okay. I got ya."

His warmth chased away the dank cold and musty smell away. In the darkness, I didn't mind smiling at the thought of being in his arms again, and I was so glad he couldn't see me grinning there. And I thought, *what the hell*, so I leaned my head against his shoulder. Then, with a *boom*, *creak*, and flash of light, the bulkhead door was yanked open, and Cheddar stood staring down at us from the bright sunshine.

"Why'd they send you to do this?" Cheddar said to me. "It's gross down here. I keep telling Gran she needs to get a couple of cats. Pike and I will get the chairs." I climbed up the stairs into the bright sunlight, and Cheddar stomped down the wooden steps to help Pike.

"Oh, there you are," Pepper said, as if I had been hiding somewhere. She had two buckets, one full of rags and another with soapy lemon-scented water.

"We gotta clean these chairs. Toilet industry people can't sit on dirty chairs," she said and tossed me a rag. I couldn't tell if she was joking.

Pike dropped the first six chairs in front of us, and then he avoided me for hours. I wish Dad had sent me to Romance Camp because I had no idea what to make of any of this.

When we finished cleaning chairs and the tables, it was time for showers. This time, there were an aunt and uncle in "my" guest room, so I was escorted to the girl cousins' room and had to wait for one of the two attic bathrooms just like anyone else.

Back in the Alden days, these two big rooms had been a long corridor of many smaller rooms where the servants suffered in the summer heat and froze in the winter. The Tooheys took out most of the walls to create big rooms for the cousins to share and one for the cedar-lined clothing archive.

A long row of windows let in the light and gave the cousins a view of the lawn and ocean on one side and the driveway on the other. All the windows were open, and overhead fans kept the air moving.

Mismatched beds and bureaus—furniture hand-me-downs from generations of Tooheys—were lined up in rows along the walls. Pepper got the only double. But it was only fair, as she was one of the oldest kid cousins and was there the most.

"Put your stuff on a bed and claim it before some Connecticut cousin gets it," she said. "That way, if you decide to stay over, you won't get stuck with a wonky one."

I looked around.

"Pick this one, so we can talk all night,'" she said. I dropped my duffle onto it (with a change of clothes and my bathing suit, but not pajamas because I didn't know this was an overnight) and lay down to wait for my turn in the shower.

"What are you studying in the fall?" I asked her.

"Liberal arts. It really doesn't matter," she said.

"Oh sure. You are going to work for the Company," I said. That's how they referred to their family business—"the Company," as if they were talking about the CIA.

"Not if I can help it," she said with a smirk. "I am doing liberal arts because I don't want my schoolwork to interfere with my equestrian schedule."

"Oh wow," was all I could think to say in response.

"I am only going to college because I found one with a great equestrian program."

"I am going to—"

"I know. You've got a full ride. I'll be riding, but you've got the full ride," she teased, but not in a mean way.

"We can hang out on the holidays. You'll have to come visit us at home."

A Connecticut cousin finally came out of the girls' bathroom.

"Took long enough," Pepper said as a greeting. "Go ahead, you can go first," she said to me.

There was no geranium soap up here for the kids, just plain white soap. I showered, got changed, and then fell asleep while I waited for Pepper to take her turn in the bathroom.

Cheddar's voice woke me, calling from the landing.

"Hey, get up, you guys. Let's take the *Ballcock* out to the island. It's getting way too Connecticut around here."

The lawns of all three houses swarmed with guests. The family was there, but there were also business associates, politicians, and all kinds of toilet industry people. They even invited my dad, which I thought was really nice.

My dad, Pike's dad, and Uncle Chet talked for about twenty minutes about the summer they had spent picking blueberries together. Dad really looked short standing next to them, with his chicken legs sticking out of his khaki shorts. Then, they had nothing more to say to each other. And then I don't know when, but he must have left at some point, because I didn't see him again.

I have no idea how long he stayed because Pepper, Pike, Pixie, Cheddar, and I took off on the *Ballcock* and spent the afternoon splashing around the cove and lounging on the island beach.

We didn't come back until after six; we were hungry, tired, and sticky with sea salt. Climbing back up that green wedding cake hill, that's when I saw him, silhouetted against the magnificent sky. I had never seen him before. There were lots of new people there, but this guy stood out. Clearly a Toohey from the hair and jawline, but just better put together than any of the rest of them.

It had to be Scout. And he was every bit as handsome as I had heard. One by one, he was embraced by the clan. Pepper and Pike ran up to meet him. I don't know why, but I stayed behind.

I looked away and watched a seal offshore for a little while, and when I looked back, Scout was gone.

"Please tell me we are not related," said a voice from behind me. I turned around, and there he was, even more handsome up close.

"No, we are not related," I answered stiffly, like a robot.

"We are not related," he repeated, pleased.

"I'm Scout," he said, offering his hand.

I know, I nearly said out loud. I shook his hand, and the breeze carried his cologne toward me. If it was cologne, or maybe some other lovely posh soap. It was clean and cedary. Maybe a little spicy, too. I don't know. It was just a good smell. I leaned in just a tiny bit to get another whiff. Maybe it was just his natural scent.

After a pause, I remembered to introduce myself too.

"I'm Claire. A friend of . . ." *whose? Pepper's? Pike's?* " . . . of the family," I finally said.

"Oh, a friend of the family," he repeated, taking my words and putting them in his mouth. It felt like it was the sexiest thing anyone had ever done to me. Actually, it was. Which really isn't saying much, come to think of it.

"Scout, have you met Flipper?" Pepper said, bounding down the hill like a golden retriever.

"They call you Flipper, eh Claire? I guess that means we're going to keep you," he whispered so that only I could hear.

"Did Uncle Finn tell you he took us on a shark dive?! We handled the chum!" Pepper said, throwing her arm around me.

"Chum? So that's what I keep smelling!" Scout teased.

"Nu-uh. That's the smell of your own breath blowing back in your face!"

"You're going in the drink, Pepper Toohey!" he shouted and stepped toward her, then chased her around the yard.

I turned and looked at the village across the harbor as the sun was setting. All my life, Dad and I had gone down to the village on the Fourth of July to see the fireworks. Somewhere, over there on the library lawn, he'd be sitting with Flo and Ebbie later tonight. He said that was the best view. We took turns getting there early to claim the spot. That meant one of us had to get there around lunch, set up the chairs and blanket, and then Flo and I would sit there all day, defending it from nervy tourists and the few unsportsmanlike locals who thought nothing of kicking stuff over and stealing a spot. I used to pick out a good book to save to read on the Fourth while we held the spot. Flo would knit. This was the first year I didn't have a Fourth of July book. And I didn't even know what Flo was knitting, although it was almost always something for me.

That's what I used to think of as a fun Fourth of July.

But we had been wrong. The best place to see the Keech Harbor Fourth of July fireworks was at the Toohey compound.

The harbor lay before us, filled with bobbing boats, floating parties everywhere. Little eruptions of laughter echoed along with the clanging sound of lines hitting masts on the sailboats. Beyond that, the village, fringed with pines, seemed like a movie backdrop.

"Why do we always have to sit out here by the lighthouse?" Pixie whined.

"Because it's far enough away from the Connecticut cousins that they won't want to join us, but not so far away as to be rude," Pepper said.

"I don't like it over here. I think the lighthouse is haunted," Pixie said.

"Oh please," Pepper said.

"I've seen lights!" Pixie said.

The sky darkened to a majestic purple, and over the familiar silhouette of Keech Harbor with its duet of church spires, now darkened to just outlines, Roman Candles and Chrysanthemums from private illicit fireworks blasted their fleeting colors, appetizers for the show to come.

The Tooheys did have the best view of it all. Well, it's only fair. They donated most of the fireworks.

From the blanket, I watched the light show, but mostly, I watched for Scout, because he was just so gorgeous. And when the sky lit up with a really bright display, sometimes I saw him looking back at me.

CHAPTER FIFTEEN

I was glad when Dad picked me up after the fireworks. I really didn't want Scout to see me the way I looked when I slept over there. I never did my hair or wore makeup anyway, but at least at home, I had some eyeliner and mascara. And I could blow-dry the weird cowlicks out of my hair.

I kept pathetically close to the phone the next day. I desperately wanted to be invited to Hazard Point.

I watched the clock all morning. I didn't want to be left out of a sail or a swim, especially if Scout was going to be there. Who knows how soon he would be going back to DC? The phone finally rang around 10:30.

It was Pixie. Pixie?! I tried not to sound disappointed.

"Hiya! Remember, this is our day!" Ugh! I forgot she had dibs on me. She went on. "I thought it would be fun if we had a reading party. Would you like to come over and read together? I have a reading cottage."

I had never heard of such a thing.

Of all the Toohey invites, this one would normally have appealed to me most. By this point in a typical summer, I would have been halfway through my reading list, and now, I didn't even know where I had left that macroeconomics book. Yet here I was, disappointed.

I had hoped we'd go out to the island. Or play baseball on the west lawn. Or scrape guano off the dock with Pepper, Pike, and Cheddar . . . and Scout. I knew that none of them would be a part of this "reading together" thing. I can't imagine any of them reading anything that hadn't been assigned.

But Pixie had "dibs." Which was creepy and cute at the same time. She was really nice, if socially awkward. That's probably what they said about me, too. She was probably someone I could have been friends with all throughout high school. Maybe she had been as lonely as me all this time, too. Probably not though, as her whole clan was never too far away.

"Sure," I said. I doubted another offer was coming anyway.

"Great! Let me give you directions. You know we don't live at the Big House. We live a few houses away. It's a similar style, architecturally, but ours has attic dormers where the Big House has a full story on the third floor. But they are both gray cedar shingles with white trim," Pixie said, who must have thought these details would be more helpful than, I don't know, a house number?

"Okay, so you go down Hazard Point Road, but not all the way to the end—wait, are you walking or are you driving? Can you drive? I don't know how. I could have gotten my learner's permit, but I have to confess I am a little afraid. It seems like such a huge responsibility to drive a car, I mean—"

"I'll be walking," I said. Dad had already left, so it was up to me to get myself into town. It would take me about an hour and a half! And there wasn't a sidewalk anywhere until you got into the village.

"Okay, so don't go by Hazard Point Road. Go to the path that comes out behind Mulligan's market. The one with the Queen Anne's lace, near the dumpster; the other one doesn't go anywhere. Follow that until it comes out on Hazard Point Road, between a privet hedge for that *bed and breakfast . . .* " she said it like it was a swear. " . . . and the stone wall for Cousin Mickey's place. Take a left and walk past three houses. When you come to the house with the dog that barks really loud, don't worry about the dog because even though it sounds like he is coming at you, he can't leave the yard; he'll get a terrible shock. They have one of those fence thingies. That's so mean! I could never. Ours is the next house, number 56."

Why she just couldn't say go to 56 Hazard Point Road is beyond me.

I took a shower and blow-dried my hair, using the round brush like it said to do in *Seventeen* magazine. It came out perfect. I looked like a shampoo commercial.

I left a note for Dad and put my good sneakers on and headed out. I hoped to run into Flo or the mailman or someone who'd drive me to the village. But the mail had already been delivered, the roads were quiet, and then I remembered it wasn't one of Flo's days with us.

On this side of the highway, we did not get the refreshing sea breeze. It was hot, and I started to sweat, and the shady areas were full of bugs.

Finally, I could hear a car coming—a big, beat-up green Plymouth. It was Skanky Stacy, my lab partner from high school who would make me do all of the work while she told me stories of her partying. I never thought I'd be happy to see her. She stopped, and I got in. In a town like Keech, we all help each other out, even if we can't stand each other.

"You going to the village?"

"Yes."

"Me, too. Work?"

"No, friends."

"Oh, yeah. You're friends with the Tooheys. Hop in. I am surprised you're going like that," she said. I got in and pulled down the visor to take a good look at myself in the little mirror. My hair was a mess. The style had fallen out, and the mousse I had used to style it was just making my hair look dirty. My eye makeup was completely smudged all over.

"God," I said. She pulled a ponytail holder off of her directional signal lever and handed it to me. I destroyed what was left of my hairstyle by pulling it all back and up into a high pony. In my shorts pocket, I found an old tissue that had been through the wash and survived as a hard white ball of paper. I used that to scrape off the black goo from around my eyes.

I asked Skanky to drop me off at Mulligan's. When she had driven off, I found the path with the Queen Anne's lace.

I got to 56 Hazard Point Road, and Pixie met me by the front gate. It was beautiful. The gate, I mean. The house was beautiful, too, but the gate was something else. It had an arch that was laden with pink climbing roses, just past peak, so that the path was strewn with fallen petals, and every little gust of sea breeze tossed more to the ground around us.

"I used to call this a pink blizzard when I was little!" she said, as the wind lifted another load of blossoms off the plants and threw the petals around us.

"Come around back and see my reading cottage. It used to be my dollhouse."

I followed her down a path flanked by flower and herb gardens. In the rear of the house, overlooking a rocky cove stood her reading cottage—a one-room gray cedar building facing the Atlantic with white trim, two windows, and double doors. It matched the rest of the houses in the compound. Two more windows were on either side. A clothesline connected it to the main house like an umbilical cord. A clothesline! They were full of surprises, these Tooheys.

The cottage sat on the path that connected the Toohey yards and traced most of the outer outline of Hazard Point. It would have been a great hiking path, but the only people who knew about it lived on it and they liked to keep it that way. I am sure they would shoot a bed-and-breakfast guest if they saw one.

Pixie opened the double doors, and a little light went on at the corner of the cottage roof.

"That's how my mother knows I'm in here. Of course, I don't really need it anymore. I am not a child, but she likes to know where I am just the same. Plus, if she knows I am in here reading, then she just sends lunch down and I don't have to go up to the house."

Pixie left the two big doors open, filling the inside with natural light and a fabulous view of the water, framed by stunted pitch pines and wild roses. In the corner, there was a little round cafe table, adorned with an old tablecloth and a mason jar filled with roses, Sweet William, and heliotrope.

A comfy wingback chair and a chaise lounge cozied up the place. Pastel patchwork quilts were folded neatly on the backs of each. Above us was a loft, accessible by ladder, where I assumed you could sleep. And the fairies and elves would fly up to the loft and cover you with a blanket made entirely of rose petals and sweet dreams. Not really, but it felt like that.

"Sit wherever you like," she said.

I picked the chair. She sat on the chaise. I looked closely at the quilt on the chair nearest me. P.E.T. was embroidered on many of the squares.

"PET?"

"Perpetua Elizabeth Toohey—my initials. These quilts were made from my childhood dresses. My mother embroidered my initials on all of my dresses." I took a close look. Tiny floral patterns, checks, and teeny animal prints filled each square of the quilt on my chair.

I had never seen any object so sweet and wonderful. I couldn't even remember if I had met Pixie's mother. And why would they even call her Pixie when she already had an adorable nickname made right from her own initials?

"I have a confession," she whispered.

Good God! *What could this be*, I thought.

"That your name is really Perpetua?" I asked. She chirped a couple of giggles.

"You are *sooo* funny! Not that, but—" she leaned toward me, "I have *never*, not even once in my whole entire life," she paused, "read *Pride and Prejudice*!" She covered her hands with her mouth and leaned back and then bent forward toward me, giggling and chirping like a bird.

"Me neither!" I said.

"Oh my gosh! I was hoping so because I was thinking, let's read it together!"

I hated reading with the class; I always read faster than everybody else. And she wanted us to sit and read together? But how could I say no when so little had been asked of me and they had all been so generous and nice to me?

"Sure!" I said, and she immediately produced two copies.

"I always buy two of all the great novels. Because I have always wanted to have a friend to read books with. Pepper only ever wants to read horse stories, and Pike prefers spy stories, and Cheddar, forget Cheddar. I asked him what was on his summer reading list, and he said the repair manual for the *Ballcock*'s engine." She paused and rolled her eyes and went on. "When I saw that book you were reading on the day we met," *good thing she didn't look inside* "I said to myself, 'Pixie, this girl is going to be your reading friend.' Do you love book sales? I haunt book sales! And now we can go to them together all winter when everyone else goes home!"

That would have been fun. But I was off to college in the fall. What a shame we hadn't met sooner.

I had never read with anyone like this before, but I was surprised at how often we reached the end of the pages together, how often we laughed or gasped at nearly the same time. Before long, I heard a little squeaky sound. I hoped it wasn't a mouse in her sleeping loft, but then it was followed by a gentle jingle of bells.

"Lunch already? Time flies!" Pixie got up and went to the window that faced the house and lifted the screen. She reached out and pulled in a vintage clothespin bag from the clothesline, then retrieved a second one. Each had jingle bells sewn onto it, and each contained a lunch. They had made their way down to the reading house on the clothesline floating across the lawn from the kitchen of the main house, where bluebirds and butterflies had helped her mother pack them. Not really, but it felt like that.

"Let's see what Mama has made us." Inside the clothespin bags were two rolled sandwiches; each was gift wrapped in wax paper and a vintage cloth napkin. Each was also packed with a bottle of ginger beer and a brownie, also wrapped in a napkin and still warm from the oven. Pixie set the table from a set of mismatched dishes that were stored in a bin beneath the table. I imagined she hosted tea parties here as a little girl and wondered at what age she got to use real dishes. Maybe she was still throwing tea parties.

"I hope you like hummus. I didn't even think to ask. Mama makes her own. It's very good, but if you don't, she'll make you something else."

"I love it," I lied. I had never had it. I wasn't even sure what was in it. I hoped it wasn't some kind of pâté. It was some kind of pâté, but it was made with chickpeas, not goose liver, thank God. It was tasty but had a weird texture. We finished eating and left the mess on the table. I wondered what kind of magical creature would come to clean it up; I suspected it was some cleaning lady, who now had to bus a table of dirty dishes in a toy house in addition to all her other duties.

"Someone's coming!" I don't know how she knew, but she leapt up and cleaned the table, placing all the dirty dishes in a different bin and stowing it back under the table, where it was hidden by the floor-length tablecloth.

"Maybe it's a gentleman caller," I said, trying to be funny. But around the corner came Scout. I felt the sweat release into my arm pits.

"So this is where you ladies have been hiding all day. Have I missed the tea party?"

"Tea? There can be tea!" Pixie shouted and jumped up. I half expected her to curtsy, having spent the morning—mentally anyway—in well-mannered Regency society. In a flash, she went running toward the house. I felt bad for her because I knew he was just teasing.

Scout reclined on her chaise and picked up the book.

"*Pride and Prejudice.* Tell me, Miss Claire, who is more intriguing to you: Mr. Wickham or Mr. Darcy?"

I took a breath in preparation to give him my very well thought-out and impressive opinions on the subject.

"Your answer had better be 'Mr. Toohey,'" he said.

I just sat there dumbfounded, and he got up and left. After a few minutes, I heard some gentle clinking, and there was Pixie with a tea tray, this one set with good china—Royal Albert Old Country Roses, to be exact. There were pretty little cookies arranged on a paper doily on a dish.

"Where did he go?" she said, holding the tray and looking bewildered. I had a feeling a lot of women asked this about him.

CHAPTER SIXTEEN

I was lounging at home watching *The Price is Right* the following week when the phone rang.

As soon as I answered, Scout just started talking.

"So, let's pretend that you live in Washington, D.C., and I've just met you at a cookout on Maryland's eastern shore . . . Some fat cat, muckety-muck's place on the waterfront. I get my assistant to find out your number. I call and you say, 'How did you get my number? It's unlisted! How dare you call me!' and I tell you that I have connections."

I giggled. I couldn't stop myself.

"You call me stalker, wacko. I say, 'yes, I am a stalker, a wacko.' You go out with me anyway because you cannot resist my charm and good looks. Then we date for eight months before I bring you up to Maine to meet the family. Gran opens your mouth up and looks in with a flashlight to check your teeth."

"Yeah," I said and giggled some more.

"So, let's pretend." He cleared his throat.

"Um, hi Claire, I don't know if you remember me. My name is Scout Toohey, and we met at Senator McMucketty's Fourth of July bratwurst party."

"I am afraid I don't remember you," I said and giggled some more.

"I was the incredibly handsome one. You couldn't take your eyes off me." I knew he was trying to be funny, but that part was true.

"Oh, yes. Now I remember you now," I said. "You spilled your drink."

He laughed. "Oh, now you're playing. Good . . . I was wondering if I might take you to dinner."

"That would be lovely," I said. "I'll have to check my sched—"

"Great. I'll pick you up at seven."

"Tonight?" It was Tuesday. I thought he'd want to go on Saturday. I never thought of any great romance starting on a Tuesday, but then again, he was here on vacation, and every night is Saturday when you are on vacation.

"Yeah, you do eat every day, don't you? You're not one of those I-think-I-forgot-to-eat girls?"

"No," I said and giggled again.

"Remember, we're not ready to go through the whole family thing, so don't say anything. Or they will all want to go with us."

They did usually travel in a pack like wolves, that was true. I didn't want Dad to know either, so I sent him into town for ice cream at 6:45, then left a note saying I was going out with Pepper. I hated to lie to him, but I was afraid he might say something to Uncle Chet or the elder Pike.

I had no choice but to wear my blue linen dress. I hadn't bought any new clothes for the summer. Hanging out with the

Tooheys, I hadn't needed any. He pulled up in a dark blue sedan, one of the family cars that seemed to be owned by no one in particular and driven by everyone. I wondered where we'd go. I had imagined us in every restaurant on Water Street, trying to figure out where we'd go, but instead, we left town.

He took me to the House of Pizza in the next town over. He had a beer, and I had a soda; they both came in red plastic cups. They were textured and felt a little greasy, even though they were still warm from the dishwasher. They had the same ones at Keech Harbor House of Pizza.

He was wearing khakis, a Harvard T-shirt, no socks, old boat shoes, and a Rolex. I had never seen one before, except for ads on the back cover of the *Bee*. I kept trying to get a look at it to see what all the fuss was about.

"Are you sure you don't want a drink?"

"Yes." I'd be humiliated if I got carded.

"So tell me all about Claire Hart."

What was there to tell? I wanted to say I was class valedictorian, but that sounded so high school, and what with drinking soda and the recent tea party, it would all make me look like a baby.

"I'm going to college in the fall." I wanted to brag about my scholarship, but it made me sound poor, so I shut up.

"What are we doing at college in the fall?"

"Finance."

"Impressive. You're a numbers girl. Math was your best subject."

"No, they were all my best subjects," I answered truthfully. "It took me a long time to decide what to major in. But I picked finance in the end. You can do a lot with money." What a stupid thing to say. Look who I was talking to.

"Smart thinking."

He excused himself and went to the bathroom. A man came out from behind the counter and came to the table with the pizza. It was Steve from Keech Harbor House of Pizza!

"Hey slacker! Why aren't you working for me this summer? I had a nice job waiting for you, Claire," And then he whispered, "What the heck are you doing here with that a-hole?"

I didn't answer. I was just so surprised to see him.

"Do you work here, too?" I asked.

"Just bought it from my uncle," he said.

Scout came back just then, so fast that I wondered if he had even bothered to wash his hands.

"Steve, my old friend," he said, draping his arm around Steve and hugging him. "I didn't expect to see you here."

"I bet not, Scout, my old friend. I own this place now, too. Bought it last year when my uncle decided to semi-retire. He lives in Greece all winter. And of course, I still help my parents run the shop in Keech. But you, you have it made. You are a mover and shaker. How are things in Washington? You must be breaking hearts left and right," he said, grabbing Scout by the chin and shaking his face back and forth.

Scout laughed a fake, forced laugh.

"We went to school together," Scout said. I was sort of surprised. I never thought of Steve as being anywhere near my age. I mean, Scout was older, but not *that* much. I had only ever known Steve as someone who worked at the pizza place. And since I had never seen him in school, I just assumed he was a lot older than me. I never realized he had been in prep school all that time.

"Steve!" a female voice called from the kitchen.

"Good to see you," he said and left.

"Sorry about that."

"Sorry about what?"

"He's . . . never mind."

Scout seemed troubled. He ate quickly, and then we left. I wondered if I did something wrong. But we made out in the parking lot until they closed. So I guessed I had done something right.

CHAPTER SEVENTEEN

Wednesday was long and quiet. No one was in town. Pepper, Pike, and Cheddar were back at home, living their regular lives in town for a few days that week. They weren't due back until Thursday.

The phone rang a little after nine in the morning. It was Flo. She'd be a little late. Whatever. Then it rang again around noon. Wrong number. Then I thought I heard it ring, but it was just the wind chimes on the back deck.

The phone finally rang on Thursday morning. It was Pepper. I was disappointed.

"Hey you!" she yelled. "Get down here." So I started down there, walking, of course.

I walked for about ten minutes when Tim drove by.

"On your way to Hazard Point?" he said.

"Yes." It bothered me that everyone knew my business.

"Hop in."

I got in the passenger side of his dad's pickup.

"Hey, I'd really like to hear about your shark trip," he said as we pulled onto Water Street. Dad must have mentioned it to him.

"Sure."

"Maybe we could get a pizza or something, and you can tell me all about it," he said. That would be kind of nice, we'd always been friends, but I didn't like that idea . . . Steve the Pizza Spy would see us and then tell Scout.

"I'm off to college in the fall. Studying marine biology," he said, so proud of himself. I used to be proud of him, too. Now he just seemed annoying.

"I know. I'm kind of seeing someone, Tim."

"Oh. I hadn't heard that."

"Not everything in this town is public knowledge," I snapped.

"Yeah, but you'd be surprised at what is. Be careful," he said as I got out of the car on Hazard Point.

CHAPTER EIGHTEEN

It started to rain as I walked up the driveway to Grannie's. Big drops hit the dusty gravel driveway, creating a low mist. Lightning flashed, thunder followed, and Pepper called out to me from the sun porch. I let myself in and joined them on the porch, settling on the wicker couch next to Pepper. She, Pike, Cheddar, and Pixie were lounging across the old wicker furniture like laundry.

There was only one television in the house, an old black-and-white set with an antenna they called "rabbit ears" sitting on top. Grannie kept it in a closet, in case of important news like a hurricane coming or Watergate. She didn't believe in kids wasting a summer day watching TV—even a summer day that poured buckets. I wished I had stayed home. We had good reception up on the hill with our aerial antenna. It had never occurred to me to invite them over to our place.

"Game? Now that Claire's here?" Cheddar asked.

"Sure. You go get it," Pepper said.

"Monopoly? Clue?"

"Clue has cards missing. Monopoly," Pike said.

We gathered around the wicker coffee table while Cheddar set up the board. Most of the tokens were missing and had been replaced by other objects. Half the money was missing and had been replaced by homemade versions drawn on loose-leaf notebook paper.

Pepper doled out the tokens because they all had their favorites. Pike got the ceramic owl, a prize from a box of tea. Pixie got a pewter pixie, Cheddar got a Lego man, and Pepper got a horseshoe charm.

"You'll have to use Scout's four-leaf clover," she said, handing me a green plastic thing. I took that as a sign.

"Where is Scout?" I asked as innocently as possible.

"I dunno. Probably mooning over a townie girlfriend somewhere," she said.

What did that mean? Was I the girlfriend? I couldn't ask anything else.

Rain pelted the windows, coming in through the screens. We had to shut the windows quickly, and soon, it was uncomfortably warm and clammy. Cheddar turned the fan on, which sent the paper money flying.

"Shut it, Ched!" Pepper yelled, then "Whose turn is it?"

"I don't know."

"Didn't somebody buy Oriental Avenue?"

"Whose house was this?"

"Ugh. This is so boring!" Pepper finally said.

"We could go over to my house," I said, finally offering. It was safe. Dad was at work. Flo did the shopping yesterday, cleaned this morning, and had the afternoon off. There were plenty of snacks, and our meager two and a half bathrooms would be in good shape.

"Let's go," Pepper said.

Pike folded the game board in half and poured all the pieces back into the box.

"You better put that back better than that. Grannie will freak if she sees it like that," Pixie warned.

"We'll do it later. We're going to Flipper's before she changes her mind," Pike said. Cheddar got the keys to the blue station wagon, and we went out to the driveway. The ancient wagon was the beach car, and it was full of sand. It was the only one they always had permission to use. Probably because it couldn't go very fast, and it was big enough for all of them.

"Keep going," I said, guiding them out of town and into the woods. After we drove by a handful of modest 18th-century capes, my mother's dream home stood out like Meredith in her designer dress at the Admiral's ball. The glassy front was angled like the prow of a boat, pointing toward our distant water view.

They got out and gawked at the big glass front, which was spotless as usual. I led them up the stairs to the deck and used the front door, which we never used. We usually came in through the garage. But I didn't want them to see that mess, with the snow shovels still out and ready for use in July and the pile of shoes and boots, all dusty and cobwebby.

It may have been a monument to modern vacation architecture on the outside, but on the inside, it was still filled with all the family things from the old house. It was one place on the outside and something altogether different inside.

I pulled the door open and let them in the entryway, which led into the living room. Its open design was well lit this time of day, even on a cloudy day, and it was cool from the high ceilings. It was quieter here, away from the winds and the gulls and the constant splashing of the surf—just the steady pounding of the rain.

But it smelled of Flo's "Refrigerator Soup." That's when she cleaned out the fridge and made soup in the Crockpot. She must have come by after I left.

I thought they'd make a beeline for the TV, but they all scattered. Pixie went to the bookshelves. Pike went to the framed antique map of Keech Harbor. Cheddar opened the lid of the Crockpot and took a deep breath.

"Smells good," he said.

"Ugh. Don't even. Tastes like a bucket of hot compost." I said.

Pepper examined every little thing. Every trinket and tchotchke and all the photos that lined the walls.

"You're in the DAR?!" She found a photo of my grandmother with her lady friends in the Daughters of the American Revolution.

"No, my nanna was. My dad's family has been here for ages."

"But then you could be in the DAR, too."

"I suppose so."

"Perfect."

"What?"

"Nothing."

"I won't join though."

"Why not?"

"Because my mother wants me to."

"Ha. I get it. I never do anything my mother wants me to."

"That's because you take your marching orders from Gran," Pike said. I hadn't realized he was listening.

"What's with him?" I whispered.

"He's still sore about Meredith. She shit-canned him. Ha!"

"I had forgotten all about her."

"I wish he had, too. Where does she live now?" Pepper asked.

"Meredith?"

"No, your mom."

"Boston."

"Hmm."

"That's far," Pixie said, joining the conversation. It must seem really far for Pixie, who was never more than a few minutes away from her own mother. I wanted to think that was sad, but really, it sounded lovely.

The boys were settled on the couch. Pike was reading *National Geographic*. Cheddar was leafing through my yearbook.

"Will you show us your room?" Pixie asked.

"Sure."

We climbed the stairs, passing more pictures. I never realized they were mostly of me before. So many had me holding a trophy or ribbon or some other award. With Pepper and Pixie examining each and every one, they felt like bragging.

Suddenly, my room felt juvenile. I had a twin bed. Holly Hobbie bedsheets. They were hand-me-downs from some friend of Nanna's. She had said "These will last longer than anything you buy today! And look, she's just as cute as ever."

"Look how neat your closet is!" Pixie said, looking in my open closet.

"I like to organize it." That was true, but it was Flo that kept it neat and full of clean clothes.

"Yeah, no wonder Gran loves you. Wait till she hears about the DAR thing." Pepper said.

"Is she in the DAR?"

"In her dreams."

I heard the television go on and someone flipping through channels.

"Wait, who's this guy? You have a boyfriend!" Pepper asked, pointing to my prom picture. It was in a plastic five-by-seven frame that sat on my desk.

"Just my prom date, Tim. Not a boyfriend," I said.

"You went to the prom! Was it romantic?" Pixie asked.

"No. And it was a big waste of time and money. I didn't want to miss out, so I was really glad when Tim asked me. But he wouldn't dance. No one at our table danced. They did set fire to the centerpiece, though. I dumped my water glass on it, which made a big stinky mess. And everyone at the table was pissed at me . . . Probably because I called them immature jackasses."

Pepper laughed at this, and I finished the story.

"Then they all got up and left us." It had not occurred to me that it was such a lousy time until I heard myself describe it.

"Where was it? In the gym?"

"What? Real high school isn't like *Grease*, Pixie," Pepper scolded.

Like either of them would know what real high school was like.

"It was at some wedding hall," I said, remembering the awful chicken and the cold macaroni with red sauce that tasted like ketchup.

"Hey! We better get going!" Cheddar called upstairs.

"Oh yeah, I forgot. Scout's taking us out to dinner," Pepper said, and my heart leapt until she added, "I guess we'll see you tomorrow."

They all thanked me for having them over, then filed away down to the blue station wagon, leaving me alone in the living room as big raindrops drummed against the huge windows. I watched them go down the driveway and vanish.

CHAPTER NINETEEN

Dad got home late, surprised to see me.

"I got dinner in town," he said and sniffed the air. "I smell soup. Ugh. I'll have to bury that in the backyard before she comes to clean tomorrow. You want some of this?" he said, handing me a box from Keech House of Pizza. I opened it and ate the few slices that were left. Such a far cry from whatever the Tooheys were doing with Scout. Dad watched TV with me for a while. It was just like my summer nights used to be, but now sitting and watching *Jeopardy!* with my Dad seemed like a punishment.

"So good to have you home for a change," he said. But he was soon asleep, snoring on the couch, and I could barely hear the contestants over him. The phone rang. It was probably for him. Everybody for me was out having a nice dinner together.

It was Scout.

"Hey."

"Hi."

"Finally got rid of them. Never seen kids take so long to eat a GD pizza," he said.

I never felt so left out of anything before.

"Can I see you?" he asked.

"Now? It's . . . it's after nine."

"So? It's not a school night," he whispered those words into the phone like going out tonight would be the most irresistibly scandalous thing I could possibly do.

What would I wear? What was clean? What was cute? Was it still raining?

"Okay."

"Great. I'll be there in ten minutes," he said and hung up.

"Dad, Dad, I'm going out with Pepper for a little while," I lied. I don't know why. Maybe because I was still seventeen and Scout was already out of college. I had a feeling Dad wouldn't approve, even if he was the shiniest Toohey of them all.

"Okay, sweetie," he said, falling back asleep, this time, falling over, with his head landing on the couch cushion. I grabbed my purse and snuck down the steps quietly to wait outside. I didn't want him waking back up and changing his mind or anything.

A few minutes later, I saw headlights and Scout pulled up in a Saab with Virginia plates. This must be his car. I climbed in. I felt like a million bucks.

"So," he said and leaned over and kissed me. I felt the Rolex band brush the side of my face as he ran his fingers through my hair. And then he backed out of the driveway.

"Let's get ice cream," he said.

"It's kind of cold. It's raining pretty hard. The Dairy Dip has no indoor seating." That was a blessing when I worked there. That job was bad enough. Imagine having to wash down tables, too! We just shut the windows, turned out the lights, and let the raccoons and seagulls clean up outside.

"You're right. Let's skip the ice cream," he said. I thought that meant we'd get a coffee or something at the Sugar Shack. But instead, we drove out to Fort Point. My dad and I often drove out to Fort Point in weather like this to see the waves. But during the day, when you could actually see them. The rain was clearing out, and the waves were intense from the storm and somewhat lit from the gibbous moon.

I got out and let the wind toss my hair about. When I was little, I imagined it was possible to cast a spell on a night like this. The sea was loud—frightening, but thrilling. Scout came up behind me and put his arms around my waist, and we walked closer to the water. A huge breaker hit the rocks, slapping us with cold water. Excited cries echoed from around the parking lot.

"I wish Flipper were here!" I heard Pepper shout. Scout heard it too. His arms dropped.

My eyes followed the sound of that voice. First, I saw the tail end of that enormous blue wagon, parked near some other cars. Then, on top of a rock on the highest point, there they were. Pike, Cheddar, Pepper, and Pixie. Pixie was shouting Shakespeare at the wind:

> *Double, double toil and trouble;*
> *Fire burn and caldron bubble.*
> *Fillet of a fenny snake,*
> *In the caldron boil and bake;*
> *Eye of newt and toe of frog—*

"Gross, Pix!" Pepper shouted. "You can't eat a clam but you like poems like that?"

"Hey, look!" I said to Scout, but he grabbed me by the hand and pulled me back into the car.

"We gotta get out of here."

"Why?" I waited for an answer.

"Because they'll never let me have you all to myself," he said, kissing me quickly, then peeling out.

"Promise me you'll have dinner with me next week when they go home. Do you like the Dock n' Dine?"

"Uh . . . " I didn't dare get caught in there with him.

"Captain's Catch?"

Yes, that would be much better.

CHAPTER TWENTY

When Scout picked me up, I let Dad see the car come down the driveway, but I didn't tell him it was a date.

"Who's that now?" he asked when he didn't recognize the driver.

"Um, I think it's Scout," I said.

"Scout. I didn't realize he was in town."

"Yeah, I guess he is,"

"Well, where are you going?" he asked. Suddenly he cared.

"Just to hang out with the Tooheys as usual." Tooheys, Toohey. What's the difference if there were five, fifty, or just one.

"O-kay," he said slowly, staring at the car in the driveway, the unseen driver sitting motionless, the motor running.

"See ya!" I shouted and ran out the front door.

Scout had the good sense not to kiss me in the driveway but reached over instead when we pulled out onto the road. He held my hand as we drove the few minutes back into town, by the collection of the little shops and right by the Captain's Catch.

"Hey! You passed it."

"Don't worry. I promised you a Captain's Catch dinner, and you are going to get one, but yours will be at the very best table in town."

I wondered if we were headed for the compound. Had the cousins gone home? Would Grannie be there? Probably the table on the patio outside the living room was the best table in town.

But no, we went right by the Big House. I snapped my head around as we passed its driveway. It was the last house on the point.

Scout slowed the car as the road narrowed. The asphalt gave way to rutted dirt, and maple branches choked with bittersweet reached out to grab at the car as we drove on.

I sat up straight in the seat, peering out the windows.

"What's the matter? Don't you trust me?"

Did I?

We came to a rusty chain-link gate across the road. Scout got out and moved the chain that made it look locked and opened the gate. He shut the headlights off, and we drove in. The vegetation soon gave way to the mowed field around the old lighthouse.

"Are we supposed to be in here?" I asked.

"Relax," Scout said. "We're in the process of acquiring it."

"I thought someone was going to turn it into a bed and breakfast?"

"As if Grannie would allow that to happen. Can you imagine? No, she put me on that right away."

"So your family owns it now?"

"Not yet."

"So it's still 'No Trespassing. Property of the US Government'?" I asked.

"Yeah, but it's okay."

Scout got out, and I stayed in the car for a moment but felt stupid, so I followed him into the lighthouse.

He lit a candle, then another, and another, and a lantern, and soon, I could see he had set up a table for us, with flowers, fine china, and a view that spanned the harbor out to the ocean.

He opened a cooler that was on the floor nearby.

"Still warm," he said and presented me with a foil take-out pan from the Captain's Catch. I opened it. Calamari. He handed me another. Eggplant parmesan. And another. Spaghetti bolognese.

"What's the matter? Don't you like Italian?"

"Something doesn't seem right. Is that all there is?"

"How many dinners did you want?"

"Well, the eggplant comes with garlic bread. Where's that? And where's the sauce for the calamari? And it's Tuesday . . . what did they do with your free mozzarella sticks?"

"What—do you have the whole menu memorized?"

"Yeah."

"Oh."

"Wait a minute. Are these leftovers?" I asked, considering the small portions.

"No. Yes. Not really. I took Gran there yesterday for dinner. I ordered extra knowing I was going to see you. Anybody can take you to the Captain's Catch. I wanted to make this special. Have a romantic dinner here away from everyone. So while we were there yesterday, I ordered some things to heat up for tonight. I knew that I wouldn't have enough time to get all this ready and get the food and pick you up . . . Come on, it's getting cold, and I have no way to heat it up again."

The eggplant parm was good, but not the calamari, which never tastes good on the second day, no matter what you do to it.

"Memorizing the menu. You're not like other girls," he said to me.

"How's that?"

"Other Keech Town girls might be saying, 'oh, take me to the compound, when can I meet your family.' Things like that. And you're not dropping a mint on new clothes. I've seen you in this blue dress how many times now?" He said and stuffed a wad of spaghetti in his mouth.

"I have already been to the compound, and I already know your family." I had nothing to say about the dress. I had no choice there.

"Yes, of course. Don't get me wrong, I like that about you."

I thought it was a rude comment. So I thought I would ask a rude question of my own.

"If you are the oldest, how come you are not going to take over the Company?"

"Ha. Well, that's a good story," he said, refilling my wine glass. "I got a 'get out of jail free' card."

"A what?"

"Yup. Once that Harvard acceptance letter came, I was excused from service. I got the fast flush to freedom," he said and laughed. "And the Harvard thing was a total fluke."

"How so?"

"I go into the SATs, and I sort of know some of the answers. My dad was all about me going to Catholic college, so I had no motivation to do well on the tests . . . about ten minutes into it, I start just filling in random circles. I stopped reading the questions! And lo and behold, I get 1520! That plus family connections got me into Harvard. I only stayed a year. Finished up at University of Rhode Island. Don't tell anyone my secret. I have a reputation to protect."

"Oh, I know."

"Yeah, what do you know?"

"You're the golden boy. There's a story in town that you stopped traffic on Water Street with your looks."

He threw back his head and really howled.

"I know exactly what you are talking about. It wasn't me they were stopping for. It was a turtle. There was a turtle in the middle of Water Street! I would have picked it up, but it was a snapper."

We both laughed and he was about to move in for a kiss when I noticed police lights on Water Street. Across the harbor, they seemed like little more than just another twinkling light, but they were blue and seemed to be floating silently through town.

"That's weird," I said, pointing to the lights.

"Probably a drunk tourist."

"Nope, looks like they're heading to Hazard Point Road."

"Shit!"

He blew out the candles and the lantern and stacked the china plates with the food scraps still on them, wrapped everything in the tablecloth, and shoved the whole thing with a big clank into the cooler, and then threw the still smoking candles in on top.

"Get in the car," he shouted, and I ran outside and got in the passenger seat. He tossed the cooler in the back, and it landed with a loud crash of its contents—I hoped that wasn't the Alden's heirloom dinnerware. We drove out, leaving the gate wide open. He sped through the vegetation, which scratched the pretty finish on the car.

We were just passing the driveway to Grannie's house when the police car came up in the other direction. Scout waved to the officer, Tim's dad, who slowed the cruiser and rolled down the window.

Scout stopped the car and opened his.

"You see anything out here tonight? We had a call about lights on out at the lighthouse. It's probably nothing, but I figured I'd better come out here and see, since it was more than the usual one or two calls. Usually, it's your Aunt Pixie who says she sees lights."

"Take that with a grain of salt."

"We usually do. No disrespect."

"None taken."

"But tonight, there were about five calls, and the Feds are twitchy about this land, so I figured I'd better come and make sure the kids haven't found a new place to get drunk."

"I appreciate that. Whew, that's all we need."

"No problem. Goodnight, Claire," he said. And with that, we drove off in our respective directions.

"You said it was okay for us to be out there."

"And it was. We didn't get caught."

"It wasn't my idea to go there! Generally, when a man asks a woman out to dinner, she can safely assume they're going to a restaurant, not trespassing on federal land."

We sat in silence for a moment as the car rolled along Hazard Point Road.

"Take me home."

"Are we having our first fight?"

"You really *are* an a-hole."

CHAPTER TWENTY-ONE

"*We missed you the* other night!" Pepper shouted over the phone. "The waves at Fort Point were unbelievable. Why aren't you here yet? We want to go to the beach."

"I can be there in a couple of hours."

"Why so long?"

"I have to walk."

"Oh. Yeah. Of course. Sorry, that was stupid of me. Cheddar, go get Flipper," I heard her say as she hung up.

I changed into my bathing suit and threw on a T-shirt and shorts over it. And I packed a bag with the usual beach changes—towel, bathing suit—plus a toothbrush, the blue linen dress, sweatpants, sweatshirt, another T-shirt, because I never knew what I was getting into with the Tooheys.

The blue station wagon careened down the driveway just a few minutes later. I got in and sat on the big bench seat. I hadn't been alone with Cheddar since we had our "yeah, I dunno" talk on the *Plunger*.

Cheddar waited for me to put my seat belt on. Then he started the car and placed his hands in the ten-and-two position on the steering wheel before executing a careful five-point turn and proceeding out of the driveway. We said nothing to each other on the way, but it was okay. Every once in a while, he'd look over and smile (if the traffic permitted), showing his tiny little jack-o'-lantern teeth.

The gang met us in the driveway and loaded up the way back with a cooler and tote bags full of blankets, towels, and rafts to inflate. Pike got in the front seat, and I shifted over toward Cheddar. Pixie and Pepper got in the back, but then Pepper climbed over the seat into the front and squeezed in between me and Cheddar, pushing me into Pike.

"Why am I back here all alone?" Pixie cried out. Pike got out and got in the back with her.

"I want the window," Pepper said to me and crawled over me, elbowing me in the face. I had enough, and so I climbed over the bench seat and into the back and ended up sitting between Pike and Pixie, with my legs splayed over the hump in the floor.

I was surprised we weren't heading for our tiny town beach. People still liked to sit there even though it was stony and too cold for swimming for most people. Instead, we headed inland to a lake two towns over, famous for its warmer water.

The lake was bustling with summer people and local families. There was a playground and picnic tables and a wide sandy beachfront that was freshly dressed with new sand they trucked in each summer and raked every week. Cheddar carried most of our stuff to the beach and set up our blanket, arranging our cooler, towels, and bags around its perimeter. After we blew up the rafts, we floated around in the water.

"We should have invited you the other night," Pepper said. "Scout said he was taking us out to dinner, but we only went to the holy House of Pizza, then he took off somewhere, and the four of us went down to Fort Point and watched the big surf."

"We were stupid. Because we can't hang out tomorrow because of the wedding," Pixie said.

"Ugh! That wedding," Pepper said, totally deflated, and slapped the water's surface. "I forgot all about it."

"Who's getting married?" I asked, half-praying it wasn't Scout, although I didn't know why I would care since I hadn't heard from him since I called him an asshole.

"Some kind of cousin."

"Julie's our first cousin, once removed," Pixie corrected.

"Then once-remove us from the guest list, puh-lease," Pepper said, then brightened. "I know! You could go as Pike's date! Pike, you had a plus one."

Once again, I was swept up in their plans.

CHAPTER TWENTY-TWO

The next morning, the Toohey wedding caravan departed
Hazard Point, beginning with the massive Suburban and the old
blue station wagon leaving from the Big House. Uncle Chet drove
the Suburban with Grannie riding shotgun and a large lady, who
I assumed was Aunt Velveeta, sitting in the backseat knitting.
When she smiled at us, she had the same tiny teeth as Cheddar.
We followed in the old blue wagon with Cheddar driving. Cheddar
had personally detailed it. The car was completely sand-free. Every
scrap of paper, every ice cream sandwich wrapper, and even the
chocolate stain on the back seat had vanished. The duct tape on
the front seat had been scraped off and replaced, so that no sticky
surface remained to adhere to an unfortunate butt. Once again
wearing my blue linen dress, I rode in the back with Pike. Pepper
sat up front with Cheddar. As the cars passed the driveway to
Pixie's house, she and her family waited to join the motorcade in
some old jalopy straight out of *Chitty Chitty Bang Bang*. At first,
I thought her mother was driving, but she was clearly reading a

book. She looked lovely with her blonde wispy bangs and curls poking out from underneath a huge hat.

Then, I realized the steering wheel was on the opposite side and that her dad was driving. He was another blond. His hair was thick and wavy, and he wore it flopped diagonally over his tortoiseshell glasses. He smiled at us. He looked like a total fop. I tried to imagine my father dressing like that, with a big wave of hair swooping down over one eye. Pixie and her family look like a cute set of dolls. It all made sense when you saw them all together. She was wearing another one of her retro outfits; this one made her look like the key witness in an Agatha Christie mystery, a young woman in peril from a killer still at large.

"Speed up, Ched, don't get stuck behind that thing," Pepper said. Pepper, on the other hand, was wearing a floral sundress with such resentment that it looked like the dress might burst at the seams out of pure fear.

Cheddar moved the car forward just a touch faster, closing the gap so they'd have to get in line behind us. By the time we made it off Hazard Point Road, we were six cars strong. We drove to Cape Avery in an orderly ride. We parked on a side street and joined the hordes of Tooheys pouring into the bride's side of the church.

I had never been in a Catholic church before. There was a lot to look at. I walked down the long center aisle, gawking at the stained glass and the gruesome, life-sized Jesus hanging on the cross behind the altar. Then I tripped over Pepper. She seemed to be squatting down before she got in the pew.

"Did you drop something?"

"Genuflect," she whispered.

"Huh?"

"Kneel down, and make the sign of the cross," I just stood there. I didn't know what that meant. I thought she'd be angry, but she was gentle.

"The sign of the what?"

"Just kneel fast and scoot in." I sort of squatted and then kneeled next to her in the pew.

"I didn't realize you weren't Catholic," she whispered. "Just follow me, do what I do. You'll be fine." *Do what I do?* What was there to do in church?

We were, of course, sitting way up front. The whole second row was reserved for us, just behind the bride's parents. Grannie sat up front with them, along with Uncle Chet, Aunt Velveeta, and the Old Salt—Pepper's dad—and her mother. I always thought of Grannie as Pepper's mother, so I was surprised to finally meet her mom. However, I was not surprised to see that she had a chunky gold horsebit bracelet, horsebit hardware on her boxy purse, and horsebits and horseshoes swirling around on the scarf tied to its handle.

A small eternity later, after kneeling, sitting, standing, singing, and receiving Communion even though I wasn't supposed to (but Pepper said I could), the ceremony was over. The bride and groom walked down the aisle, and the church emptied out behind them, each row filing out on cue. Pike offered his arm, and I took it. With the recessional playing and everyone looking at us, it was fun to imagine we were the bride and groom, walking arm-in-arm amid smiles and good wishes . . . until I saw Scout sitting in the last row laughing with some blonde who had a face as flat as a frying pan.

I ignored them and walked straight out of the church, gripping Pike's arm a little tighter.

The wedding guests made quite the spectacle. Two hundred or so well-dressed people filed out of the church, following the bride and groom and wedding party, walking two-by-two down a busy street in the height of summer toward a grand old hotel in the center of town.

Some tourist aimed her disc camera at us, and a flash went off.

"I think they might be Kennedys," she told the man with her.

"Smile big, she thinks we're Kennedys," Pepper said loudly, pulling sunglasses from her pocket and putting them on.

We found our table at the reception and sat down. Surrounding my plate was a shining arsenal of silverware, each with its own archaic and specific use. I knew just what to do, thanks to Flo.

After my mother left and my grandmother died, I wouldn't eat. Flo tried all sorts of tricks to get me to eat: Bugs Bunny flatware, toast cut into shapes with cookie cutters, *au gratin* everything, food hidden in mashed potatoes (treasure pie, she called it), chocolate chips in my cream of wheat. It wasn't because I was upset about my mom or that I wasn't hungry. I just liked saying no and then watching her jump through hoops to please me.

Then one day, I came down to lunch, and there was my teddy bear wearing a tie, seated at the dining table, which was covered in my grandmother's good linen tablecloth and my toy tea set laid out for a formal dinner for two.

"Madame President, you are dining with King Teddy of Beartopia."

That's how I learned what fork to use when. Flo knew all about table settings, because in the Alden days, when there was a whole slew of servants taking care of the family in the house at Hazard Point, Flo's Aunt Mildred was one of them. They had an actual dinner gong, and when the butler rang it, the Aldens went upstairs and dressed for dinner. Mildred served at the table, in addition to a lengthy list of other jobs that fell under the description of "maid" back in the Alden days.

Mildred taught Flo how to lay a formal table, just like Flo taught me with a toy set. We had to pretend things were different sizes, and of course, there wasn't an oyster course, just a mini marshmallow. Sometimes, Ebbie or my dad would join us for lunch, and Flo would really make it fancy with sherbet between courses and a variety of glassware.

The first course arrived. Oysters.

"Which one?" Cheddar whispered to me.

"The one closest to Pepper that isn't hers," I whispered back.

"Thanks," he said, lifting a glass of water.

"Not yours . . . and you're welcome," I said absently, taking my glass from his hand, while I scanned the room for Scout.

As I guided Cheddar on his forks and knives throughout the meal, I felt I could draw a straight line between all the events in my life and that reception, as if everything I had learned—from those tea parties to years of enrichment camps—was preparing me for the Tooheys.

Cheddar was on one side of me, and some unknown, bucked-toothed cousin in a big hat was seated next to me. Although Pike and I had walked in arm in arm, he ended up directly across from me at the large round table. Pepper was not happy about the seating arrangement, and although she made a stink, she got seated too late to do anything about it. The groom's relations we were seated with weren't at all interested in being bossed around by her the way her own cousins were. She did find a bartender who didn't card, so that was a great consolation for her.

Scout was a few tables away, with that pan-faced girl laughing at all of his dumb jokes.

I couldn't help but stare. Even her front teeth were flat, and she showed them off with a big smiley-face grin. It was like her mother had spent her entire pregnancy on her stomach, face down on the pavement, with a pile of encyclopedias stacked on her back.

Cheddar once again made it his business to make sure he danced with all his girl cousins (and me) an equal amount of time. This time, Pike refused to play along and sat there, staring off into space, refusing to dance with anyone—not even the good-looking guests on the groom's side. Scout kept off the dance floor, too. But he was there with that girl, no question about it. Pixie did a swing dance with her dad after Pike refused her.

Eventually, it was just Pike and me sitting across from each other at the table. I caught him looking at me over the centerpiece, then he looked away quickly. He wouldn't even talk to me. Was Meredith supposed to be his plus one? Was he suddenly sore about that again? Was he mad at me for it?

The band played "Always and Forever," and then suddenly, he was standing beside me.

"Would you like to dance with me?" he asked, as if we had just met. I couldn't tell if he was nervous or just asking because he felt like he was supposed to. I nodded, and he took me by the hand to the middle of the dance floor. I felt his wonderful strong arms around me, and I didn't care why he asked. The chatter and color of the room began to fade away until it was just me and Pike and the music.

Then, there was an obnoxious blast in my ear of a man belting out the lyrics.

"*Each moment with you!*" It was Scout's voice, and it was followed by Pan-Face's cackle.

"Oh my gawd, stawp it!" she shouted.

"*Is just like a dream to me!*" he continued, and then Pepper joined him, and suddenly, I was no longer dancing with Pike but linked arm-in-arm with Pike and Pan-Face in an ever-growing circle of cousins, then aunts and uncles, the new in-laws, and even Grannie and Uncle Chet and Aunt Velveeta, swaying back and forth, shrieking the lyrics so loud we couldn't hear the band and ended up a half a measure ahead of them. The lead singer dedicated the next song to the bride and groom, who were going on an extended honeymoon where they'd be volunteering on an archaeological dig in Turkey. And so they played that awful "Istanbul (not Constantinople)" song. I had to leave, because once I heard it, it would get stuck in my head for days. Flo listened to that sort of old stuff when she mops the floor. She had a little boombox that plays the mix tapes that Ebbie makes for her. She also had a Teresa Brewer tape, but I hated that one so much I hid it behind a bookcase, which proved she never cleaned behind there.

I snuck outside to the patio, joining the smokers. A clutch of old geezers with cigars were perched on the wicker lawn furniture, puffing away. I found an empty bench with a nice view of the marina and wondered how long I could get away with sitting here alone. I wondered if they would forget all about me and return to Keech. I wondered if I had a dime to call home. I wondered what Dad would say when he had to drive all the way to Cape Avery to get me.

"Whatcha doing?" That voice in my ear. It was Scout again, hanging on the back of the bench. "Hiding? Hiding from me?"

"I hate that song."

"You're not very romantic," he said, climbing over the bench and sitting next to me.

"You think that's a romantic song?"

"Well, it depends—" he started to answer.

"There you are!" It was Pan-Face. She flopped down on the other side of him.

"Hi, I'm—" Just as she said her name, a tray was dropped in the kitchen, and the sound of the crash blasted out the window. I could have sworn she actually *said* Pan-Face.

"What?!" I asked.

"Janice. I'm Janice."

"Flipper." I shook her hand.

"You Tooheys sure are a ball with all your nicknames," she said.

"Can't imagine what they'll call me!" she laughed. I fake smiled. She tugged Scout back inside by the hand, and they disappeared in the crowd.

She thought I was a Toohey. Imagine that. Scout didn't correct her. Imagine that.

"Ugh. Moon Pie sure keeps Scout on a short leash," Pepper said as she sat down beside me. That was when it hit me that you might get a nickname you didn't know about.

"Let's blow this clambake," she said.

"Gladly."

We rounded up Pike, Cheddar, and Pixie, who, by then, had enough of looking precious with her parents and was eager to leave with us. We told Grannie we were taking off. She said that it was okay, so I guess what we were really doing was asking if we could leave.

"Let's go to the outlook!" Pixie said. We piled into the car, and Cheddar drove as we took in the sights. He pulled into the parking lot for the short hike up Cobb's Mountain. We hiked in our good clothes and bare feet. From the summit, we watched the sun go down until the chill sent us back to the car.

"Put the heat on, Ched. I'm freezing," Pepper said, undoing her seatbelt and turning around.

"Sit down and put your seatbelt on," Cheddar said.

"In a minute. I have exciting news," she said, pausing for effect. "Three words. Sainte Anne de Beaupré."

"That's four words." Pixie said.

"It's early for the pilgrimage," Pike said, suddenly shedding his mopey mood.

"When?" asked Cheddar.

"Next Thursday, coming home Monday. It's a shrine in Quebec," Pepper said, suddenly remembering I wasn't Catholic. Would I need a passport? Was I even invited?

"Well, that clogs the pipe," Pike said.

"That's hardly any prep time," Pepper said.

"It's doable," Cheddar said.

"You'll come, right?" Pepper said to me at last.

"On a pilgrimage?" I asked. Was I ready to go full-on Catholic for the Tooheys?

"No, you goof. Gran's going to the shrine," Pepper said. "We're going to have a party. The Party. The one we throw at Hazard Point every summer when she goes to Quebec. Since oh-so-responsible Scout's here, she's going early so he can keep an eye on us while she's away. Isn't that just a hoot? He's the one who invented the Sainte Anne de Part-tay."

CHAPTER TWENTY-THREE

The following Saturday—the night of the big party—
was also my birthday. Flo baked my favorite chocolate cake, and
she and Dad and Ebbie gave me a few thoughtful gifts. I didn't
want to make a big deal out of it, and I definitely didn't need
anyone else to know. A little part of me would have been happy to
stay at home and watch a movie on the couch, like we usually did.

I asked Dad to drop me at the Keech House of Pizza and told
him I was meeting up with Pepper for a slice. I couldn't risk him
all of the sudden deciding to come say hello to the family at the
Big House. I went in, watched him drive off, and then walked the
rest of the way to Hazard Point, taking Pixie's short cut through
Mulligan's parking lot.

The first thing I noticed were the cars. Lots of cars. Most I
did not recognize. The family's collection of sedans was lost in a
sea of fancy foreign cars. It looked like a Stockholm car dealership
with all the Saabs and Volvos—and Meredith's BMW. What was
she doing here?

I was overdressed. Way overdressed. I had gone into town with Dad and finally bought a new dress. *What was I thinking?* Damn, Scout had me all turned around. I was about to leave to go home to change when Pepper saw me. Oddly, she looked overdressed too—for Pepper that is—in the most wacky way. She was wearing gobs of black eyeliner and a black tank top and a short denim skirt. I don't know why I noticed, but she had actually shaved her thighs. She had missed a small rectangle of blonde fuzz above her knee.

She was draped across some beer-swilling lunkhead in a varsity lacrosse T-shirt.

"What—did you just come from church?" she asked me, clearly already drunk. And the party had barely started!

"Meredith's here!?" I half asked, half reported.

"Yeah, she's just trying to make Pike jealous with that loser," she said, pointing to the beautiful six-foot-two man that Meredith was wrapped around. "He's so over her," Pepper shouted in Meredith's direction. I debated telling her about the hair on her leg but decided she shouldn't be anywhere near a razor in that condition.

Pike wandered into the kitchen as if on cue. Pepper put her arm around me and Pike.

"Why don't you two just go upstairs and make some beautiful blond babies," Pepper said.

I blushed immediately. I had never seen her like this. I had seen her obnoxious (daily), and I'd seen her drunk (more than once), and I had also seen her both obnoxious and drunk. But this was a whole new level. It was like the part in a movie where the tourist visiting the quiet, quaint village finds himself in an archaic pagan ritual.

"Get a brewski, and come out to the bonfire," Pepper shouted as she and the lunkhead left the kitchen. I pictured them throwing furniture on the bonfire, hauling Toohey heirlooms out the glass sliders and into the fire pit. "Sacrifice another Chippendale chair," she'd probably shout.

Just then, I saw two figures run along the upstairs hallway.

"What's down here? More bedrooms?" one said. All I could think of was the Alden emeralds, just lying there. So I rushed up the stairs.

"Excuse me, may I help you?" That's what we say around here when we really mean: *I am noticing that you don't belong here.* The couple slid to a halt.

"We're just looking around," the boy said.

"The upstairs is closed to visitors." I don't know what made me think to say that, but it worked.

"Uh, we're sorry. We didn't know," the girl said, and they came back down the hall. I stood halfway up the grand staircase at the landing where it turned, hands on hips, and watched until they got all the way downstairs. I chased Sailor Moon out of Grannie's room and then locked the door. I am sure there was a key somewhere.

"Brava, my lady." It was Scout; he stood at the top of the stairs, clapping. "Defending the castle already."

"Shut up."

"I am serious. Thank you for doing that."

"I didn't want them rummaging around your Gran's room with the Alden emeralds just lying there," I said.

"Jeez. Good call," he said, suddenly sounding sincere. *This is what it's like being part of this big clan*, I thought. *Someone always has your back.*

"Keg's broken!" came a shout from the kitchen.

"I better get that keg fixed. That's what a chaperone does, right?" Scout said and winked, grabbed me by the hand, and pulled me along with him down the stairs and into the kitchen. Cheddar rushed by us.

"I'll do it," he insisted. The big farm table in the kitchen where we had chopped potatoes for chowder was now filled with stacks of pizza boxes, open bags of chips, and towers of large plastic red cups. Chips crunched beneath my feet as I walked through the room. I leaned against the counter next to Scout. Although I was still mad at him, I didn't know where else to be. I was afraid of super-drunk Pepper. And I was more afraid of that crowd at the bonfire.

"Come on, Ched, you're usually handier than that," Scout said as Cheddar fiddled with the keg. He poured a few cups, then it broke again. And again.

"Aw, come on!"

"I can't fix it with you all staring at me. Come back in twenty minutes," Cheddar said.

"What's the matter? Is it empty? Should I order another one?" Scout offered.

"Absolutely not," Cheddar said,

"Well, fix it. Flipper hasn't even had a drink yet."

"It's okay, I don't want any," I said.

"That makes two party poopers. Cheddar won't drink tonight either. Maybe you should have gone with Grannie," Scout teased.

"It's just not my kind of party. Not how I had hoped to spend the night."

"What? This is the best party of the summer. Sainte Anne de Part-tay! Only comes around once a year, like Christmas . . . but without Midnight Mass," Scout said.

"Yup. But it's my birthday," I blurted out, wishing I had stayed home and had too much cake with Dad, Flo, and Ebbie.

CHAPTER TWENTY-FOUR

"*I wish I had* known! No, this is no way to spend your birthday!" Scout said, in a serious tone.

I was grateful for this.

"Let's get out of here."

"You're supposed to be chaperoning," Cheddar said.

"Really. You're nineteen, diaper baby. Do you still need a babysitter, Mr. Party Poopy-Pants?"

Cheddar shot us both dirty looks.

"I am not going anywhere with you," I said.

"What? Are you mad at me? Are you breaking up with me?" I was surprised he was talking like this in front of Cheddar.

"What about Janice?"

"Janice? Is that what this is about? She's just . . . Janice. We've known each other forever . . . I got the invitation for the wedding before we met, and I needed a plus one, and she mentioned she was going to be up here anyway. It never occurred to me to tell you because it wasn't any kind of date. And I didn't expect you to go to some boring old wedding for someone you didn't even know." Now that he mentioned it, I felt weird that I had gone.

"And I couldn't un-invite her, that would have been really rude."

That was true.

"Cheddar, man, what the frig are you doing to the keg?" some boy said, pushing his way into the kitchen and then stumbling over to me.

"Hey, you're new," he said and elbowed his way between me and Scout. His sweatshirt was damp and orange with cheesy dust. He filled the space between us with the stench of beer, Cheetos, and his stinky armpits.

Scout pushed the guy out of the way and wrapped an arm around me.

"Scram," he said, and the guy left. "But what the frig are you doing to that keg, Ched?"

"Breaking it. This party is out of control. You should have gotten the half-keg like we asked," he said to Scout. "These kids are shitfaced."

"*These kids are shitfaced.* Buzzkill." Scout mocked. "Let's get you out of here, birthday girl." He opened a cupboard and grabbed two champagne flutes from the top shelf.

As we slipped out the kitchen door to the garage, Cheddar whacked the tap with a crab mallet, breaking it for good.

Scout handed me the flutes and lifted a tarp to reveal an old refrigerator hidden among the Toohey fleet of bicycles, which included everything from minuscule tricycles to a bicycle built for two. The fridge was draped in a chain and secured with a bicycle combination lock. Scout flicked the dial quickly and opened the door wide enough to extract two bottles of champagne.

"The Toohey wine cellar," he joked. "Come on, we can't have you turning magical eighteen in this mess," he whispered.

"Where are we going? The lighthouse?" I asked. Even though I wanted to stay mad at him, I could feel all traces of the anger melt away.

"Nah, can't get in there anymore . . . and we can't really go far . . . I would have taken you out to dinner had I known, but I am supposed to be chaperoning this shindig . . . I know." He took my hand, kissed it, and held it as he led me out of the garage and through the side yard, where the mop-headed hydrangeas and towering rhododendrons muffled the sounds of the party. It must've been glorious when those rhododendrons bloomed in spring. I had to make sure to notice next year.

We walked along the footpath that traced the compound, and the noise of the party was replaced by the normal sounds of a summer night on the point—the rolling of the waves, the crickets and night birds, and the gentle swish of pitch pine branches in the breeze.

An archway had been cut into a thicket of beach roses and, bending low to avoid the nasty thorns, we stepped through and found ourselves in Pixie's yard, right in front of her reading house.

He tried the doors to her little hideaway, and they were unlocked.

"Perfect," he said. He dropped my hand to open both double doors, and the full moon filled the little house with a delicious silvery glow. He put one champagne bottle down on the floor and popped the other open, sending the cork out the door and over the gardens.

"Whoops!" he said. Little moths started to gather at the light on the roof.

"How'd that go on?"

"It goes on when the door opens. That's how Pixie's mother knows to send her lunch down." I chided myself for knowing that answer. It made us sound like babies playing with dolls.

"Huh" was all he said, and he closed the doors to see if the light would go out. It didn't.

"Huh," he said again. "Oh, well. Lunch, you said? They won't be bothering us with any cucumber sandwiches if they are up in Quebec."

"Pixie won't like us being here,"

"Little miss Pixie is shitfaced, and last I saw, she was cleaning out the tonsils of some pencil-neck geek who is as dorky as her old man. Tell me she doesn't have daddy issues," he said.

I was shocked he spoke that way about family.

I was thirsty, mostly from being nervous at that crazy party, and I drank my champagne down faster than I wanted to. The last time I drank too much champagne, I woke up in Canada. I felt dizzy and sat down on the chaise. He refilled my glass.

"A toast" he said, "to the beautiful Claire. On a beautiful night. Now, she's finally eighteen," and we clinked glasses.

"That looks comfy," he said and sat down next to me on the chaise.

"Look at all these books. Do you think that's what she does in here?" he asked, kissing my face.

"I know it is." I laughed.

"And you are eighteen and going off to college and will forget all about me."

"I will not, and of course we can see each other."

"Yes of course . . . but let's not talk about the fall right now. Right now, it's just you and me," he said, caressing my face and kissing me, sliding his hand down my leg and moving my dress up over my hips just as the doors flew open and the beams of half a dozen flashlights poured in.

CHAPTER TWENTY-FIVE

"*J knew there was* someone in here!"

Even with all those flashlights in my eyes, I could tell it was Pixie. I was so embarrassed to be in her reading house without permission.

"How *dare* you!" she said.

"Calm down, Pix," Pike said.

"Well, they know about us now," I said to Scout, but he had vanished, and I was alone in the cottage, with the cousins and assorted drunk rich friends staring at me. I stood up and pulled down my dress. I couldn't believe how high it had been hiked. And I am sure everyone saw my underpants. And what's worse, it wasn't until I jumped up that I realized that my dress had been unzipped down the back, and it fell off my right shoulder, exposing my ratty old bra. I snatched it back and was hoping Pepper would help me zip back up, but she slipped her arm around Pixie, and they walked away silently together. One by one, the party guests all followed them, leaving me alone with the moths flitting around the light. So I ran.

I ran through Pixie's yard, under the rose arch, certain it was now flowerless—just leaves and rose hips. I found the path back into town and rushed through the tall grass; the swishing noise it made as I ran past sounded like whispers. A deer crossed the path, and I jumped back, falling over into the grass, convinced I was covered in ticks. Somewhere, I had lost a shoe. I limped through the path until it brought me down to Mulligan's, smack into a bunch of stoners from high school.

"Hey goody two-shoes," one of them said, and they all laughed. Then more joined in.

"Toohey-good-shoes."

"She's only got one shoe."

"Toohey good for us," the last one stumbled to make a joke as I pushed through them, ignoring the laughter and taunts and ran to the front of the store. It was closed. I could call home at the House of Pizza. Steve would let me use the phone. Or maybe he'd take one look at me and say *I told you so*.

I couldn't run any further. My feet were killing me. I had stepped on some broken glass somewhere. Probably a bottle of cheap beer dropped by one of those stoners tonight or any other night of the year. Or any year. They'd be out there drinking in Mulligan's parking lot until they got married. Then they'd drink at home or at the VFW—and be replaced by another generation of stoners and drunks, leaving their layer of broken glass and cigarette butts in Mulligan's parking lot, a treasure trove for an archaeologist in the distant future.

I walked, leaving the smells and sounds of the sea behind, finally crossing under the state highway. Overpasses are creepy and wider than you imagine when you have to walk beneath them. Above me, I could hear pigeons cooing. I knew that meant I was walking barefoot through untold quantities of bird shit mixed in with the road sand.

I had never realized Keech Town was so uphill from the harbor road. There were no sidewalks. I thought I heard a growl in the darkness. A car passed me, turned around, turned around again, and pulled up alongside me. A Volvo with Massachusetts plates.

The driver's window came down. I looked for a house I could run to. I never realized how far apart the houses were or how long the driveways were until now. If I screamed, no one would even hear me over the television.

"Claire, get in." It was Cheddar. He was alone.

"No."

"No, really, get in. There's a mountain lion out here somewhere," he said.

"The state warden says there isn't."

"There's all *kinds* of things out here. Stuff like you wouldn't believe." I stared at him for a second.

"Whose car is this?" I asked.

"I don't know. Ours were all blocked in. This one had the keys in it, so I took it. Please, Claire. Get in the car. Let me get you home safely," he said gently. "Please. It's no trouble."

No trouble? You stole a car, I wanted to say, but I caught my reflection in the window and realized I was in no position to protest. I was a mess. My eyes were swollen and red and circled with smudged eyeliner and mascara. My hair was a nest of snarls. I was holding the only shoe I had left in my hands. My feet were bloody and dirty.

I got in and didn't even look at him. I was grateful he didn't try to talk. We drove in silence until we pulled into my driveway.

"Thanks for looking out for me," I said.

"It's what I do," he said and shrugged. I reached for the door handle and started to get out.

"Claire, wait. We're not supposed to say anything bad about family, but . . . Scout's kind of a dick, pardon my French. He's a real dickwad, and they all know it. But they'll still blame you . . . 'cause he's Scout. And Pepper always says stuff she doesn't mean. She and Meredith used to be friends, and you saw the way she treated her. It's just the way the family is. I just want you to know. I feel bad you had to find out this way."

After I said nothing in response, he said "Bye."

That was the last time I went to Hazard Point.

CHAPTER TWENTY-SIX

J threw my shoe in the trash on my way into the house. I went upstairs and flopped into bed. Dad was out, I didn't know where. I wanted to sleep late, really late, like all day, and stay numb and ignorant. But I forgot to pull the shade down, and the sun woke me up as soon as its rays hit my window at 5:38 a.m. I lay there, burning in my humiliation until I heard Flo come in an hour later. I jumped up and brought my bathroom garbage downstairs to hide the shoe before she saw it. I kept hoping that Scout or Pepper would call. That someone would tell me that I had nothing to be embarrassed about. That something crazy always happens at the Sainte Anne de Part-tay.

But no one called. Not even Pixie. I felt the worst about her. It was a real trespass, sneaking into her reading house without permission. It's something I normally would never have done. But I just followed Scout. I knew he wouldn't call.

I told Flo I had cramps so she'd leave me alone, but she knew something was up. She knew my schedule better than I did, since she was the one who washed my sheets and underwear and kept the bathroom fully stocked with what she referred to as "supplies" in a whispered tone. She left me alone and didn't ask me any questions. I wonder if she could have heard something.

That week, Dad kept offering to drop me off in the village, so clearly, he was clueless. I had to keep making excuses as to why I didn't want to go anywhere. I couldn't tell him his favorite family booted me out of their inner circle because I was messing around with the Golden Son in Pixie's playhouse. I didn't even want to admit this to myself.

I finally got my reading done. I read all about macroeconomics, and I finally read that flowery novel Dad brought home for me in June. It was about true friendship. I cried throughout most of it, and I loved it even though I didn't want to. Then I reorganized my closet again by color, just in time to pack it all up and off to college.

After three days, the phone finally rang, but it was only Tim.

"I was wondering if you'd like to have lunch together, before we go our separate ways next week," he said.

It suddenly hit me that for the first time in twelve years, I would not be saving a seat for him on the school bus. It made me sad, and it made me sadder that I hadn't even thought about it until now.

"Sure," I said.

"Dock n' Dine?"

"Maybe . . . if it's not too crowded," I lied. I just wanted to make sure it was clear of Tooheys. I was 18 now and could go to the forbidden Dock n' Dine if I felt like it.

Tim picked me up in his dad's truck, and we headed toward the village. The *Plunger* and the blue station wagon were nowhere in sight. Maybe they had all gone back to school or on some new adventure. It was a Tuesday, early in the day and late in the season so the Dock n' Dine was quiet. Soon, the tourists and most of the Tooheys would be gone for another year.

Tim requested one of the outside tables in the section close to the road, which I thought was pretty weird for a wannabe marine biologist. It was separated from the sidewalk by a low white fence. Tim sat next to it and rested his arm on the rail. I couldn't understand why he'd want to sit next to the road when there were plenty of perfectly good tables right on the water. But Tim was holding court—the harbormaster, Mulligan from the market, one of our old teachers, even a late-season tourist asking for directions, each stopped to chat as they passed by on the sidewalk. Maybe he just liked to socialize. Maybe he was showing off.

My skanky lab partner came and took our order, and even she was nice to me because I was with Tim, and everybody loved him. I started to place my order, and then out of the corner of my eye, I saw the old blue station wagon slowly cruise by.

"I'll have the garden sal . . ." I started to say. I wasn't in the mood to eat anything that might have been caught anywhere near Hazard Point.

"A garden sal-*what*?" Skanky said. She wasn't that nice.

The car door opened while it was still moving, and Pepper jumped out, stumbling a bit, then regaining her footing and storming up to the fence. She leaned over it and into my face.

"You! You ruined EVERYTHING!" she screamed. Gasps erupted from the few other diners around us. Skanky laughed.

"Do you think it was just an accident that we met you back in June? Gran saw your picture in the *Keech Town Crier* and said 'This one, Pep, get this girl. This is the one for Pike.' And then wasn't it just my dumb luck, not two days later, and there you are,

192 • The Last Summer Before Whatever Happens Next

walking down Water Street oblivious, dumb, and happy. And, oh didn't I get lucky again when you *saved* that idiot dog of hers."

"You threw her! You threw Sailor Moon overboard!" I shouted. Let everyone hear how awful she is!

"God no! What's wrong with you?" she hissed. Then she leaned in closer, baring her teeth like a threatened Chihuahua. Really, more like one of Grannie's German Shepherds.

"You were perfect. Everyone liked you. Pike, Pixie, Gran, we all did. Even I liked you. And then you had to go and ruin it with Scout! Scout could be in Congress someday. Who do you think you are? He can't get involved with some nobody from a broken home in Keech—"

"You know what? Screw you, Pepper," I said, standing up. I thought that would shut her up, but she just kept going on. Cheddar had turned the car around and now pulled up behind her.

"Pep," he said, leaning out the window, "get in the car." But of course, she ignored him.

"You would have been perfect for Pike. He's not going to Washington or Boston or even Portland, for chrissakes." she said. Pike sat in the passenger seat and avoided my gaze.

I can't believe I ever liked him or fell for Scout and his smarmy charm.

"He needs a local," she kept going, "but one that is also good enough for him. You know how hard it is to find that? But there you were. Tall, check—blonde, check—smart, check, valedictorian no less, although how hard could that be at Keech High—and local, check, check, check!"

"Let's move inside, Claire," Tim whispered. I ignored him.

"And what perfect timing! You show up just in time to get rid of Meredith." Now she was on a roll.

"Get rid of Meredith? Why do you even care?" I shouted. By now, Pike had joined her on the sidewalk and pulled her elbow.

"Come on, Pep," he urged, but she ignored him.

"Meredith. I'll tell you what Meredith is. Meredith is a rushed wedding and a baby on the way. That's how girls like Meredith operate."

"Oh come on, Pepper. What is this? 1965?"

"How do you think we got stuck with Cheddar's mom?" Pepper laughed. "Do you know why she never comes out to the Point? Because she's fat as a cow and owns a yarn shop. A *Yarn Shoppe*! With two 'p's and an e!"

"How can she come out to the Point in summer? Summer is her busiest season!" Cheddar shouted from behind the wheel of the car. "And at least my parents love each other." Pepper rolled her eyes.

I had no idea. I would have liked to have gone to Aunt Velveeta's yarn shoppe. I had seen Cheddar's mom knitting in the car with Uncle Chet. I bet Flo would have liked something from that yarn shoppe, too.

"Pepper," I said to her. "I just want you to know I wrote your grandmother the loveliest note, telling her all about the wonderful party I attended while she was away praying in Quebec."

"You didn't. You couldn't." Pepper started to hyperventilate and turned completely white. She rushed back to the car and jumped into the back seat.

"Drive! Drive!" she shrieked at Cheddar.

CHAPTER TWENTY-SEVEN

I never thought I'd hate college so much, but I did. I thought I'd want to be at a big school in Boston and be anonymous for a change. I thought I'd like being in a class where no one knew me, instead of being in a class with the same kids I had known since I was five.

At a big college, no one would remember the time I peed my pants in kindergarten, or cried because I forgot my lunch, or had a screaming fight with Pepper Toohey at the Dock n' Dine, or ran home barefoot crying from a party on Hazard Point.

But it was awful. There were over two hundred kids in my American History class. I agonized over papers only to find out they were read and graded by some graduate student who couldn't even match my name with my face. My professor called me Clara. He didn't give a crap about me or anyone else in that class. Plus, I quickly made a new list of screwups to be remembered for.

First, there was The Boyfriend. I met him on the very first day, before classes even began, during the move-in. Dad had just helped me unload everything. There was one box of books left, and I said I could handle it. He drove off, and I found out I couldn't handle the box of books, but the soon-to-be boyfriend swooped in and carried it up the three flights to my dorm room. He lived in the same building, one floor down.

From that moment, we were inseparable. We went to the freshman welcome lunch together that afternoon—and every meal after that. We studied every weeknight together. He wasn't a party animal like the Tooheys, so although we partied a little bit on the weekends, we mostly explored the city and each other.

Then, he went home for the long weekend in October, where, as his roommate told me, he called his "real girlfriend" back home "Claire" instead of "Heather" while they were "at it" in her bedroom.

Whatever the catalyst, the consequence was she came up the following Saturday and kicked my ass right in the laundry room. I was folding a load of lights when she came in the door.

"You Claire?" she said, blowing a big pink bubble and inhaling the gum back into her mouth with a loud *smack*. Dummy me answered yes. She took three long steps toward me—she was a high school basketball star and five-foot-eleven—and punched me in the face so hard I fell over into my laundry basket. Then she sat on me and pounded on me right on my own clean sheets while her friends cheered her on.

Someone called campus police, and her friends pulled her off me, and they all ran out the emergency exit. I had to walk around with two black eyes for a week—earning me the nickname "Sluggo," which stuck. The smell of fabric softener still makes me want to puke. But the absolute worst was that her gum got stuck in my hair, and I had to cut it all off. I didn't realize how beautiful it was until I saw it in a pile on the floor of that cheap chain salon, where they hacked out the giant gum wad and then tried to make a hairstyle around it—my first short hairstyle since my second-grade pageboy.

"My hair really doesn't look like this," I found myself saying to the student who checked our IDs at lunch. But it did. Probably worse in the back where I couldn't even see. The Boyfriend was history. His giantess girlfriend now came up every weekend and was a formidable presence on campus from dinnertime on Friday until eleven at night on Sundays—to keep an eye on him. Not that I wanted anything to do with him after that, anyway.

"We still have all week," he had said to me. I told him to shove it. Now I had to make all new friends and habits, since everything I had done since I had moved in involved him. But it wasn't long before a November nor'easter changed all that.

"Isn't that where you're from, Sluggo?"

I was in the common room, watching the storm on television when there it was—Keech Harbor on the Boston news.

"Tragedy struck this close-knit coastal town in the storm-related, accidental death of 58-year-old nurse Eberta Raymond, who fell off the roof of her home while clearing the gutters of clogged leaves."

Ebbie! There, while I sat in shock over the horror of Ebbie's death, from the back of the room, some guy yelled "Keech Harbor! I went to a party there once where there was this couple making out in a playhouse, and then she ran home crying in her underpants, and then I ended up doing shots with the guy."

I wasn't sad to be leaving school for a few days; in fact, I told the registrar that Ebbie was my aunt, and I was given leave till after Thanksgiving because the first holiday would be "a tough one."

Mom actually took time out of her busy social life to drive me to Portland, where she put me on the bus home.

"What a shame she won't be able to get Ebbie's life insurance or anything since they weren't married. Tell Flo we send our condolences," she said, while the car idled in front of the bus station.

"I will. I will tell the woman who raised me—that job you didn't want—that you are very sorry she can't get Ebbie's money," I said and slammed the door.

Dad picked me up at the bus stop in Freeport. Flo was with him. She just sat there in the car, like a sad lumpy old lady, staring at the dashboard. I lugged my giant duffle full of dirty laundry and tossed it into the trunk, realizing she probably knew what was in it. Dad told me that while I was home, it would be my job to do Flo's job—cook, clean, and do the groceries, while he helped her make arrangements. It was the least I could do.

Everyone says it was a blessing that Ebbie didn't suffer, but wouldn't an actual blessing have been if Ebbie had said "screw the gutters" and just let them overflow rather than climbing up there herself?

Dad dropped me off at Mulligan's with the shopping list while he and Flo met with Ebbie's sister, who had come up from Rhode Island to see what kind of house she had inherited and to remove anything valuable. Ebbie hadn't made a will, so now Flo was soon to be without the home she had known for 30-odd years.

Despite all this, it was a relief to be back in Keech. The storm had stripped every leaf off the trees, and low gray clouds sat like a lid over the quiet village, now devoid of both tourists and, for the most part, Tooheys.

Just the same, I scanned Mulligan's aisles through the window just to make sure. I went in and pushed the cart, loading it with the items on Flo's list—potatoes, turnips, carrots, butternut squash, then onto the end cap with the holiday specials, Bell's Seasoning, cans of pumpkin purée, and unbleached flour. Placing the bag of flour in the cart, it occurred to me I would be doing the baking and the cooking. I didn't even know how.

I rounded the corner into the baking aisle to get the rest of the things on the list, and *bam!* There was Grannie and Pixie by the packaged nuts. They didn't see me, and I was able to swing the cart around, park it by the office, and hide in the ladies' room.

Pixie! Of all the Tooheys, she's the one I wanted to see the least. I still felt embarrassed, and I owed her an apology for invading her private reading cottage. It was Scout's idea, but I knew better. It was wrong to be in there without her permission. Maybe we could still be reading buddies and go to book sales. But in my heart of hearts, I knew she was petty enough to never accept my apology or want my friendship back. So I sat, pants around my ankles, on the toilet, reading the graffiti on the back of the stall door—highlights included a peace sign that had been engraved and re-engraved with pen deep into the wood; the name *Molly* in childish scrawl, allegedly done by the second-grade teacher when she was a child; and, my favorite, in extra-thick black marker, *Mulligan is a cheap SOB.*

Then, the bathroom door opened, and in walked someone wearing bright red sneakers and argyle knee socks and Christmas pins on her shoelaces. And there was only one person in Keech who would be dressed like that.

First, Pixie cranked some paper towels. Then she opened the door to the stall next to me and began pulling toilet paper off the roll. But the stall had a wonky dispenser (which is why I didn't use it), and it took her forever to unroll the amount she wanted because it only gave up a couple of squares at a time. *Squeak-clunk, squeak-clunk, squeak-clunk.* She must have placed it on the seat, but it fell on the floor.

"Ew, gross."

She kicked it aside and started again.

And back to the toilet paper dispenser. *Squeak-clunk, squeak-clunk.* Then more paper on the seat. This went on and on until I felt ridiculous sitting there, but not so ridiculous to want to leave the safety of the stall. How much toilet paper did she need to protect herself from a seat at Mulligans? When she finally sat down and started peeing, I made a run for it.

And ran straight into Gran.

"Flipper!" she said. "What a pleasure to see you! I was so sorry I didn't get to wish you well before you left for college. I didn't realize you'd be heading off to school while I was away."

"Oh yeah," I said.

"You're in town for the funeral? Your cleaner, her friend? I understand they were close. Please extend my condolences. Did you see Pixie when you were in there? Pixie, come out and see who I ran into!"

Just then, I saw my dad pull up in front of the store.

"I can't stay. Lots to do," I lied. I didn't have half the things I needed in the cart. And now there was a line at the check-out! Two whole people—where did they come from?

So I left the cart by the office and ran out to the car.

"Where's the food?"

"I left it."

Flo turned around to look at me. And despite her grief, she still put me first.

"I'll finish. Is there a cart?"

"By the office door."

"Period trouble," she whispered the lie to my dad.

I lay down in the back of the car like a coward.

Dad said nothing to me because he did not want to talk about period trouble.

I got out of Keech ten days later without seeing another Toohey. I got off the bus in Boston to hear some guy shouting at me.

He was my age, nice-looking and friendly.

"Hey, where do I know you from? Did you go to Loomis? No, it's not school. I know—it's Keech! Keech Harbor, Maine, right?" I didn't recognize him. He was wearing a Northeastern University sweatshirt. But no one I knew from Keech went there.

How could he know me from Keech Harbor? He wasn't a townie . . . or a Toohey.

"Keech Harbor party, at the Toohey's. You were that girl in the pool house." I felt sick. My red face told him I was that girl, even though it wasn't a pool house. There wasn't even a pool. Dumbass.

"Hey, sorry. No offense," he said softly. "Listen, everybody has a story about that party. And no one cares. My uncle projectile vomited off a balcony, and now he's vice president of sales in Asia-Pacific for Toohey International . . . So where do you go to school? We should hang out sometime."

"No," was all I said and kept walking.

I didn't go home again until Christmas. Flo spent the holidays with us, staying in the first floor bedroom that used to be my grandmother's. To cheer her up, Dad took her ice fishing on New Year's Eve.

That was followed by snowshoeing in January, cross-country skiing in February, and then a church bus trip to see the Boston

Bruins in March. Then they golfed, mountain biked, even learned to kayak together.

"She's not my girlfriend, you know, because she's not like that." My dad had told me when he picked me up at the bus station. "But honestly, this is the most fun I have ever had in a relationship!"

I said nothing. And hoped that was all I would hear about it.

I hated my major. Finance was boring and heartless. And I began to suspect that every finance major I met had been at that last Toohey party. So at the end of the year, I withdrew. I transferred to a small school in southern Maine. I changed my major to liberal arts. Which meant I lost all my financial aid. Which meant I'd have to work my tail off all summer. And that's how I ended up back in Keech that June, working at the Dock n' Dine with Skanky as my supervisor.

CHAPTER TWENTY-EIGHT

"*It's your section, Poindexter*," she snapped at me pointing to the Tooheys filing in and filling up a table. Pepper, Pike, what looked like the current girlfriend—approved or not—Pixie, two newly promoted teenage cousins (I recognized them from last summer), and Cheddar, of course. All come to fatten up on Uncle Chet's tab. I wondered if I should send him a thank-you note for all the lunches that he didn't know he bought me last summer.

I sighed. Then I felt a firm hand grip my shoulder. It was Steve. His family had just added the Dock n' Dine to their restaurant empire.

"If you were going to work here for good, I'd tell you to go over and face them, get it over with," he whispered in my ear. "But I know that you are going to finish college. You are going to get out of this town. Maybe you'll come back once or twice when your perfect WASP husband drives you up here for a visit in your Volvo wagon with the heated leather seats with your perfect WASP kids—one of whom will look just like me. But that's a story for another day." I laughed. He was a great boss. He always got us smiling, even though most of the time, his jokes were completely inappropriate.

"So you go take that busload of cotton-top tourists coming in from Rhode Island. We'll put them on the other deck. And leave the Tooheys to me."

I took a step away, but he grabbed me by the waist and escorted me to the sidewalk to greet the tourists.

"And the next time you want to date a local millionaire a-hole, pick me," he whispered and then shouted, "Welcome to the Keech Harbor Dock n' Dine!" to the flock of old folks spilling off the bus and wandering toward the door.

"This is the lovely Claire, and she's going to take care of you. You will love her. Everyone does. She was crowned Miss Keech Town Blueberry Harvest last year," he lied.

They loved that.

"No, I was not. He likes to joke," I said.

Six of the old fellows asked me about how our *chowdah* was. What a joke, their accent is way worse than ours. I lead them over to the far deck. It hung out over the deep water in the harbor.

"Oh this is nice way out ovah the wawda,"

"Oh we'ya ovah the wawda."

"It's nice ovah the wawda."

They seemed to like repeating each other in their awful accents. They all ordered *chowdah* for starters and laughed as each member of the party took their turn ordering it. Still, I wasn't complaining. I would take a group like this any day over waiting on the Tooheys.

Keech Harbor had been discovered by tour bus operators, and this was a gold mine for the Dock n' Dine. We always put the big bus groups on the far deck. It had a view of the lighthouse, and seals would often pop their heads out of the water below. And then the bus groups would throw oyster crackers over the side even though we told them not to, and the cracker throwing wouldn't end until a gull landed on a table or pooped on someone's head. No kidding. We had at least one head-splat a week.

Steve put the Tooheys on the sidewalk side. We were separated by two sets of glass doors, the indoor dining room, and the bar. It was like they weren't even there. I couldn't even hear them, and most of the time, if I stood the right way, I couldn't see them.

I had just set down the last iced coffee for the cotton-tops when I caught sight of Pepper coming toward the first set of sliding glass doors. She yanked the heavy door aside, marched through the dining room, and accosted me when she emerged from the second set of doors, pushing me across the deck and against the railing.

"You ruined everything! Now I have to get rid of another one," she said, pointing to the new girlfriend.

"Really, Pepper," I said, "That is not my problem or my fault. I have work to do, do you mind?" I couldn't believe how calm I was!

Pepper lunged for me, but I stepped aside, and she stumbled and somehow flipped over the railing, falling with a *plop* into the deep water.

Gasps erupted from tourists, then it spread to the other deck.

Pepper splashed around and screamed, "I can't swim!"

For a split second, I couldn't believe it. But all last summer, I had not seen her swim once. She went out sailing plenty without a lifejacket—but there she was, flailing away. I threw my tray down and jumped in after her. God, the water was so cold it took my breath away. I pulled her in a rescue hold over to the dock where Cheddar, Pike, and Skanky met us. Skanky put a comforting hand on Pike's back. *Let her get rid of the girlfriend*, I thought. They grabbed Pepper out of my arms and up onto the wood. Then both boys pulled me up, too.

"Oh, Pepper," Cheddar sighed, as if it were her fault. And just like that, I was in again.

CHAPTER TWENTY-NINE

I got an invite to the First of Summer clambake. I politely declined.

I got an invite to go sailing on the *Plunger*. I said I had to work (I didn't).

Then, I got an invite to Scout's wedding. That I tossed in the trash.

"What?! You have to go to this," Flo said, chasing me around the kitchen with the gorgeous envelope now stained with tartar sauce from the takeout fish-n-chips she and Dad had brought home the night before. Flo lived with us full time now.

The house was now cleaned every day. Dad got her to give up making compost soup. And that tangle of Christmas lights, beach chairs, snow shovels, and boots that had lined the garage entrance was now neat and organized, and all the old boots I had outgrown were cleaned and donated.

"I hope the response card isn't ruined," Dad said as Flo took homemade pizza out of the oven.

"You've got to go, kiddo. Show them that bygones are bygones and that this thing with Pepper is over. They are trying to make peace. Accept the olive branch."

That was easy for him to say. He didn't know the whole story. I hoped he never did. As far as I could tell, he just thought I had a fight with Pepper. *Girl stuff*, he called it.

"You want to work in the nonprofit world? You have to get along with people like the Tooheys." Now that I was no longer a finance major, Dad had lots of advice.

"Why, just because they're rich?"

"Yeah, because they're rich. They're the ones that write big checks. Who do you think paid for the addition to the library or for the benches along the waterfront? Or that swanky public bathroom down by the beach?" he said.

"Fireworks," I added.

"The fireworks, yes, that, too. This is the way the world works. This is also your big chance to meet some important people. You never know who is going to be at that party. The father of the bride is in Congress. The mother's some kind of society lady."

"How do you know all this?"

"The engagement announcement was in the *Bee*."

That frigging thing, I thought and rolled my eyes.

"Think about it," he said. "We're going on a short hike out to Fort Point. Do you want to join us?"

I didn't. I just wanted to stay home in the quiet. But the house wasn't quiet anymore. It now hummed with the motor for Flo's fish tank pump and the bubbles it created. But it was a cheery sound. And the tank cast a welcoming glow into the living room, like the house had a heart.

Later, Dad brought the ketchup-stained invite up to my room.

"Do it for me," he said with a serious tone I had never ever heard before. He handed it to me. "I have to live in this town. I don't want anybody saying anything bad about you."

"You're worried about what people say? You've taken up with Keech's most famous lesbian and you're worried about what people say?"

"Flo would take a bullet for you. She's the most honest person I know, yet she lies for you all the time. You think I don't know when it's your time of the month? I get that it's some secret code between you for when you want to be left alone. I am not stupid. I'm a CPA. I can count to 28, you know."

CHAPTER THIRTY

The wedding was in the same town as Toohey Manufacturing. I went alone. I couldn't even dredge Tim up for a date because he was now serious about some surfer chick, also a marine biology major.

"I am going to save the dolphins," she told me when I waited on her at the Dock n' Dine. She was wearing a bathing suit top and a sarong.

"In a bikini?" I said. Tim shot me a dirty look. What was his problem? I didn't tell her that she would more than likely end up working at the trout hatchery if she stuck around here with him.

Nor did I tell her that here in Keech Harbor, we generally put on clothes when we go out to eat. I did not say these things, even though my new hobby was saying what I thought. I had been a goody two-shoes long enough. If I was going to be a waitress, I was going to be *that* waitress.

Tim's girlfriend wasn't awful; she just annoyed me because it would have been handy to have him as a date to this thing. I wouldn't have to sit there by myself, and I wouldn't have to get a ride from Dad and Flo, as I still didn't have a license.

They were more than happy to drive me, as it meant they would get a look at the Toohey's winter home. Dad slowly drove through town, taking it all in. He finally pulled over.

"So this is the church, and the reception is across the street and down a few blocks, in one of those big white mansions we went by," Dad said.

"Which one was the Toohey mansion?" Flo asked.

"All of 'em," Dad said. The two of them gawked around like tourists on a car safari, waiting to see the species in its natural habitat.

I sat in the backseat, watching the church doors.

"Get it over with," Flo said. "We're going to look at a new-for-us kayak, then we're going to the farmer's market, then we're going to the pub for dinner," she said and handed me an index card on which she had written the pub's name, address, and walking directions. "We'll meet you there. They have Irish music after dinner, so take your time."

I got out of the car and walked slowly up the church steps, timing it so I wouldn't get stuck with any ushers I knew.

Some curly-haired kid I didn't recognize offered me his arm.

"Bride or groom's side?" he asked. "Neither," I said and walked in without him. I couldn't remember when to sit or kneel or stand in the Catholic church, and I wouldn't have Pepper there to lead the way, not that I wanted her to. I sat in the back of the church with some other people who didn't know or care what to do. We all tried to follow along while the rest of the congregation stood, sat, kneeled, and mumbled their responses.

I looked over at the stained-glass window nearest to me, some tonsured monk in a brown robe. The plaque beneath it said:

Saint Vincent Ferrer Patron Saint of Plumbers
In memory of Joseph Toohey

The old ditchdigger. Which one was the patron saint of plumbers? *St. Vincent or Old Joe*, I wondered.

Many of the women on the Toohey side of the church wore fancy hats. I thought this was because they had been watching too many historical dramas on PBS, but I later found out Pepper was dating the youngest son of an English baronet. They had met riding. He had no hope of ever getting a royal title. She had no desire to ever work in the family company. They sounded perfect for each other, and it also sounded doomed. Somewhere, the baronet and lady were in attendance, and the Tooheys had been outclassed.

Up by the altar, stood Scout, incredibly handsome in a classic tuxedo. I hated that my heart still lurched at the sight of him. I hated that I hoped he'd see me there and still like me. Not that he'd even recognize me. My hair had darkened to a light brown, and after the gum incident, I started getting regular haircuts and now sported bangs for the first time in my life. I looked so different I still surprised myself when I looked in the mirror. It was the new me. I had also started flipping the bird, but I refrained from that in church. But I was flipping it big time on the inside.

Cheddar and Pike were next to Scout. Standing beside each other, they looked like a bat and a baseball: Pike, tall and blond, and Cheddar, shorter and round. The processional began and the bride appeared. Big surprise, it was Janice from last summer. Her face looked rounder than ever, framed by the giant puff sleeves and the layers of frills along the neckline of her Lady Diana-rip-off wedding gown.

A cathedral-length train trawled the red carpet as she advanced down the aisle on her father's arm, some congressman from Connecticut. That explained the television news crew outside.

The ceremony was endless—a full Mass. I got up and received Communion, because I knew Pepper would know I wasn't supposed to. I think I saw Grannie smile at this, but I was probably just imagining it.

I had hoped to escape out the back of the church, but photographers and reporters jammed up my escape plan. I had to wait for the whole wedding party to recess and the congregation to empty out behind them. So I stood there, fake smiling and waiting.

There was Scout. Dirtbag, no—what was it that Steve called him?—a-hole. He kept making this "oh-I-am-so-happy-you're here" face, even to me. And then came Pan-Face. She had no idea what kind of heel she was marrying, as she was clearly pleased as punch to be walking out of the church with him. She had four bridesmaids: two flat-faced like her, and the others were Pepper and Pixie.

I took a step backward when a photographer from the *Bee* leaned in for a photo of the bridal party, blocking their view of me. Pan-Face had her bridesmaids bedecked in mint green gowns, with ruffles and puff sleeves that were slightly less dramatic than hers. It was totally worth going just to see Pepper wear that monstrosity, especially with the plaid ribbon around her waist and the big bow at the back. Pixie would probably wear hers again on a bike ride or to pick mulberries.

I suppose, at one time, I would have thought this was great fun, and for a moment, I missed them. I missed the entire clan. Last summer, I would have had a job to do like taking care of the guest book or handing out favors. Instead, I was just another guest.

I finally got outside the church with an old lady who had sat on the groom's side. She gripped the handrail and took one step at a time. We had a quarter mile to walk to the reception, so I offered my arm to her.

"Thank you, my dear," she said.

"My name is—" I started.

"I know, dear, you're the one they called Flipper. I'm the one they call Old Pixie," she said. I couldn't help but like her.

We followed the crowd down the street, along a stone retaining wall, above which sat the Toohey mansions: three identical stately white homes across the street and slightly uphill from the toilet factory. We came to a steep flagstone staircase.

"I hate these GD stairs," Old Pixie said.

"Is there another way up?"

"It's all uphill from here, no matter how you go. You go on ahead. I am just going to take my time. Maybe I'll just find a gin mill somewhere instead."

"I'll see if I can get you someone to help."

"Young Cheddar will. See if you can find him. He's the only one with any brains," she said.

I climbed the long flight of flagstone steps to the front door of the center house. This was Pepper's real house. This was where she and Pike grew up.

It was swarming with guests and uniformed waitstaff, one of whom opened the door and welcomed me to the wedding. Another handed me a glass of champagne.

"Please go through to the backyard," he said and pointed to a set of French doors that opened to a patio.

I stepped out on the patio and ran into Cheddar.

"You came."

"I did . . . is there another way up here from the street? Your Aunt Pixie is stranded at the foot of those stairs—"

He nodded, said nothing, and disappeared.

In the middle of Pepper's huge backyard, a disproportionately large in-ground pool glimmered as phony lily pads floated on its surface. It had a tall curving slide and a three-meter diving board. I didn't think you could even have one of those in a private yard, but evidently the pool was deep enough—thirteen feet in the deep end, according to the little number painted on the side. I walked over and could feel the heat rising off the water. It was heated. So this is what they did when they weren't in Keech Harbor in the summer—and not once did they invite me to swim in this nice warm pool.

Its filter hummed along with the jazz combo that was set up in front of the pool house. They played "How High the Moon," and even though it was just the cocktail hour, a few people—old people—danced to it. That is, until the roar of a lawn mower drowned out the music, and all eyes turned toward the sight of old Aunt Pixie being towed in a garden cart by Cheddar at the wheel of a Sears Craftsman riding mower.

After a while, I found my place card and headed to the big wedding tent that straddled the property lines of the family houses. I feared I'd be stuck with toilet parts salesmen or secretaries, but they actually put me at a good table. There were three cousins from Connecticut—Bubble, Squeak, and Totsie. They were friendly, and they were fun. There were also two of Pepper's friends from school—they were as awful as her, but nice enough to me—and another girl I couldn't quite place.

"Hi," she said. That voice.

It was Skanky! Her trademark black eyeliner had been replaced by a light green. She was wearing a teal taffeta dress with a ruffled neckline. She hadn't even dressed this fancy for prom. Her bleached blonde hair had been set and teased into a massive updo.

"I didn't know you'd be here," she said.

"You didn't mention it either," I said.

I sat down.

"How do you know Pike's new girlfriend?" Totsie asked. My jaw dropped.

Skanky grabbed my hand under the table, and when I met her eyes, she begged me not to say anything.

"Everyone in our town knows everybody else," I said. Maybe now she wouldn't give me such shitty shifts.

"What do they call you?" Totsie asked.

"Stacy."

"Yeah, I know that's your name, but what do *they* call you?"

I almost said *Skanky*. But I didn't.

"They call her Sunny," I said. I knew that she wouldn't be around long enough to enjoy that lovely nickname. Pepper probably called her "Specials" or "Catch of the Day" behind her back.

Then, the bride stopped by our table and said hello.

"It is so great to see you all. Thank you all for coming." She turned to Pepper's school friends, "How were things in Connecticut? Is that candy store still across the road from your old school?" Then she turned to Skanky. "I am sorry that we've been monopolizing Pike for so long. But you're in good hands with Flipper here.

Flipper, it's so good to see you again," she said, shaking my hand. "Thanks so much for coming."

How does she even know who I was? Had she actually memorized her seating charts? I had to admit, that was impressive, even if it was as phony as all get out. There's no way she could have remembered me.

"So tell me, how did Scout finally propose?" Bubble asked—or was it Squeak?

"Oh my gosh, you know I didn't think he ever would. He was such a wild man, and I was pretty sick of waiting for him to calm the frig down. I mean, we had been on and off for years. But I knew he was the one. It was just a matter of being patient. Waiting for him to finally grow up," Pan-Face said, beaming as she watched him schmooze a table across the tent.

"You were together for years?" Bubble (or Squeak) said.

"Forever!" Squeak (or Bubble) said.

"Eight all in all. Because we met in prep school."

Listening to all this, I felt stupid and ill.

"We were at a wedding last summer. We were just sitting there in the back of the church, and he turned to me and said, 'What do you say, Janny; should we finally get hitched?'"

So they were already engaged during the Sainte Anne de Part-tay when he was climbing all over me in Pixie's doll house! What a dirtbag. Did she know? Did she even care? Would she believe me if I told her? She finished her chitchat and moved on to the next table.

"What's a Flipper?" Skanky asked me quietly.

"Never mind," I said and excused myself to go to the bathroom.

As can be expected, the Toohey house had more bathrooms than any house I had ever seen. Just the same, they were all full when I needed one. Cheddar found me pacing the hallway.

"Use the one in Pepper's room. Upstairs, second door on the right," he said and brought me to the front hall stairway and pointed up. Of course she had her own bathroom. I climbed the stairs, passing years of school portraits, cookout pictures, parties, there was me—imagine that, me—in one of those pictures hanging on the wall of fame.

I got to the top of the stairs, and there was Pepper's room. I knew it was her room because it said so on the door, with a wooden sign that had a horse and her name on it. It was so weird that, as close as we had been that summer, I had never actually set foot in her room before. It was like seeing her soft white underbelly.

Her room overlooked the pool in the back. She had a cherry-wood bedroom set: full canopy bed, desk, and bureau. Her bedspread and drapes matched, a deep navy with a red and gold pattern of foxes, hounds, and hunting horns.

She had a shelf of plastic horses, each had a doll rider standing next to it. They all had different outfits. There were ribbons and trophies—her real name is Mary Margaret—awards for horse shows, jumping, dressage, swimming—swimming? Do horses swim? No, it was Pepper. Pepper was the champion swimmer! There was a picture of her with her swim team. And another with medals draped around her wet neck.

I realized she had faked that whole drowning episode as I silently peed in her palatial bathroom. I had been played by the Tooheys yet again. I flushed and went back downstairs to get a look at this champion swimmer. There she was out there in that bridesmaid dress, her massive swimmer shoulders on display for the whole world to see and admire. How could I have not made the connection?

I saw my reflection in the hall mirror, and behind me were a group of Tooheys. Pike was one of them. I saw me and Pike, together in the mirror. It's true we would have made a beautiful couple. Pike caught me looking at him in the mirror and smiled. I wondered what it would be like to stand on my toes and kiss him. I remembered what it was like to have his long, strong arms around me. I imagined them around me as we toasted in summer with everyone looking on in approval. Wouldn't that be nice? It was probably all still mine for the taking. What the hell else would I be doing there? Just that. I was here to distract Pike from Skanky. I didn't know why. She'd make an excellent saleswoman, considering how many of her stories end with her being face down in a toilet.

He made his way over to me and kissed me on the cheek.

"It's so nice to see you again, Flipper. I am so glad you came. I love your hair." The band started playing "Always and Forever."

"We danced to this, remember?" he said.

"We tried to dance to it," I replied.

"How about it? For old time's sake." I shrugged, and he took me by the hand and led me out of the house, through the yard, and onto the dance floor. This time, we danced without Scout screaming in our ears. We danced alone without the whole family getting involved. And there I was in Pike's embrace again. He smelled like that wonderful geranium soap. I moved in closer to drink it all in.

Then I remembered Skanky, sitting there alone in some sale-rack prom dress and matching shoes that she probably spent a week's worth of tips on.

"So Stacy," I said, stepping back.

"Oh, Stacy? We're not, you know, she's just a friend."

"Really? That's not what I hear." He looked troubled.

"Don't worry," I said, "Pepper will take care of it." I was making him uncomfortable on purpose.

Then I caught sight of Grannie smiling at us. I thought about her controlling all our lives from her throne on Hazard Point. Picking out brides and grooms like dogs and bitches.

I stopped dancing and left Pike. I helped myself to a wedding favor: a box of gourmet chocolates tied with the wedding colors of white and mint green. Then I swiped a second one for Flo, and I left without saying goodbye to anyone.

CHAPTER THIRTY-ONE

The Following June

I don't mind admitting I am super nervous. It's my first trip overseas, and it's to Africa, so it's a big trip. But I better back up.

My sophomore year was so much better than my freshman year. It was worth having to serve *chowdah* to the tourists and gin and tonics to the occasional Toohey. I adored my new major—nonprofit management. It was still money and numbers, but it was money and numbers with heart. I love my new school. In fact, that's why I am going to Africa. The school has a partnership with an organization that is building a school in Tanzania. That's why I'm here at Logan Airport, with my dad and Flo, waiting to board a Lufthansa flight for Dar es Salaam, a trip of twenty-four hours with two connections. Beyond that, I'll take a four-hour bus ride into the countryside along with a dozen other college kids, hopefully some of whom actually have some construction skills. I finally got my driver's license—Flo taught me—because I thought I needed it for the trip. Turns out, what I needed was a *commercial driver's license*; that's what they mean by "CDL."

None of us have one, so we'll have to sort out a bus driver once we get there.

I'm getting college credit for the program. When we get back, we'll raise the funds to have the school furnished with desks and chairs and supplies. It is the most exciting thing I have ever done in my whole entire life.

"Ya got your sunscreen?" Flo asks.

"Yes, Flo."

"Oh, we got you these," she says handing me a little gift bag.

"Ray-Bans!"

"You've got to protect your eyes," Dad says. *Is he crying?*

We wait until the last possible moment to say goodbye.

"Your parents?" the lady asks me as I hand her my ticket and passport.

"Yes. My family," I say and look back at the people who raised me.

That full family I had always longed for—I had it all along, and now I was going far away. I don't know what is truly between Dad and Flo, and I don't care. They seem very happy, and Flo looks after Dad way better than my mother ever did. But I feel a little sick to my stomach leaving them. What if one of them falls off our roof while I am gone? I have never been out of New England before—except for that accidental trip to Canada.

I am one of the last to board, and the plane is nearly full. By some miracle, the seat next to me is empty, thank God. I flip up the arm rest and sprawl out across both seats. I know I am lucky to be a part of this trip, and it's just nerves I'm feeling. I'm happy getting away from Keech for the summer, although I'll miss the opportunity to call the cops with a noise complaint about the Sainte Anne party like I did last year.

"Excuse me, excuse me." A final passenger pushes his way down the aisle. I just know I'll lose my spare seat. Yup. Now this big guy is standing there, shoving his bag in the overhead, while his belly pokes out from the bottom of his shirt.

"Whew, so glad I made it," he says, plopping down next to me. It's Cheddar!

"What are *you* doing here?" I say it so loud I embarrass myself. The passengers in the next row glare at me.

"Going with you. I got the last spot on the team," he says, pleased with himself, as he stuffs a book called *Principles of Construction* into the seatback pocket in front of him.

"What?!" I point to the book, then I point at him. "What—what are you talking about? I can't believe this! There is no last spot on the team. I have the roster. There was no Cheddar Toohey or Chester or Chet or Chesterfield or Chicken Pot Pie or whatever the hell your real name is!"

"Michael."

"What?"

"My name is Michael. That's another reason they reject my mom. She wouldn't make me a junior. She said I should be my own person . . . " He pauses and smiles with all those little pumpkin teeth. "So anyway, I got the position funded, and *then* there was a last spot on the roster. And *then* I applied for it, and *then* I got it. And then I got my CDL so I could drive the bus," he says, matter of factly. Just like that.

"But why?"

"I was at the Dock n' Dine with my dad getting soused. Well, he was the one getting soused. I was the one who was going to drive. I asked Steve if you were working that night, and he told me that you were getting ready for your trip. He told us all about your project and the school and the kids, and I couldn't stop thinking about it. Tasmanian kids were going to get an education because of you."

Did he just say "Tasmanian"?

"I called up Scout's wife, Janice—she's awfully nice by the way. Anyway, her mom's this big fan, fill a fan, fantropist—"

"Philanthropist?"

"Yeah, that's the word. Anyway, she made a few phone calls, and here I am."

I stand up and look around.

"Alone?"

I have never seen him travel without the pack, except for that time he stole a car so I wouldn't get eaten by a nonexistent mountain lion.

"Yep."

"Shocking," I say and sit back down.

"Ain't it though!" he says with a smile. I have never heard Cheddar talk so much at once.

"You see, Claire, I had a 'come-to-John' moment of my very own this year. I don't know if you know, but Pixie got married on St. Patrick's Day. Then Pike got married in May out on the Point."

"I know. Kinda young, don't you think?" I saw the announcements in the *Bee*. Pike married a valedictorian from the next town over.

"Oh yeah, Gran's been marrying off people left and right. She's not taking any more chances. She found out about the Sainte Anne de Par-tay last year because the cops came and broke it up. Must have been the new renters in the neighborhood who called them," he laughs at this and continues.

I blush with guilt.

"Anyway, she says that this generation was too out of control, so she started marrying everybody off so they'll chill out. Both weddings were friggin' frigid. It snowed on Pixie's day—that really clogged the pipes. Two fender benders in the church parking lot. And Pike's was freezing. They had a signature cocktail—hot toddies—and Gran got totally loaded. You should have been there. It was wicked hilarious," he says and laughs some more.

I am shocked by what he finds funny. I try to picture Grannie sloppy drunk but can't.

"So I was helping Gran and Pepper and some of the young cousins put away the tables and chairs. There's a whole new crop of cousins coming up. I'm too old to be hanging around with them, and also, I don't really want to know what they're up to. So sometimes now, it's just me and Pepper—she'll be out of a job soon now that Pike's married. Gran will get a new second in command," he says and rolls his eyes.

I picture this new stranger getting those Alden emeralds and feel sorry for Pepper. She was awful, and I still hate her, but those are her family's jewels.

"Anyway, Gran says, 'It's just you left to marry off now, Peppah.'" He's actually imitating her voice. I can barely believe my ears.

"And I said, 'Don't forget about me, Gran,' and she says—I'll never forget this—she says 'Oh Cheddar, you'll just be everyone's favorite uncle.'" This time, he adds slurred speech and wobbly hand gestures to his imitation.

"And I said, 'So what am I—that unmarryable, that unlovable?' And she said, 'Of course you're lovable, Ched. I love Sailor Moon, but I am not going to breed her!'"

Cheddar takes a deep breath. I don't know what to say. I touch his arm and try to find the words.

"No, it's okay. I am glad it happened. It made me think. And I thought—what if that's not what I want? What if . . . what if I want to be a dad? What if I didn't want to be this generation's bachelor uncle? That's what they wanted for my dad, too, you know." Ched looks over at me where I sit, listening.

"Then I looked over at the west lawn of Hazard Point and saw my whole life laid out before me. Like holes on a mini golf course.

"I guess it has always been there waiting for me, but I had never really seen it before. There was me, best man at Pike's wedding earlier that day—hole one, the tee off. Then godfather at Pike's kid's christening—hole two, the water hazard. Me going into the factory on weekends because he has a family and he made a promise to a customer—hole three, the windmill. Being a Christmas guest, but never getting to be Santa—hole four. Oh, don't worry; Uncle Cheddar will take care of it. And then I will be the one cleaning up someone's messes. Just like my dad cleaned up Scout's—that's getting the ball in the friggin' clown's nose!"

I don't know what surprises me more, that he has such deep thoughts or that he expresses them in the terminology of miniature golf.

"And you know what. I realized I didn't want to play through. Then I thought about you. And how you didn't know where you were going to work after college and how you weren't even afraid of not knowing. And I tried to think like that, you know, imagine a different future." He goes silent.

"And what did you see yourself doing?" I ask.

"Nothing. I mean, I have no idea what I want to do. Maybe I will want to work in the business. Maybe I will suck it up and end up as Pike's second banana over at the Flush Factory. Maybe that will even be okay. And then I went to the Dock n' Dine and heard about what you were doing this summer and I thought, *maybe I want to go build a school in Tasmania with Claire.*"

"Tan-zan-ia," I say it slowly, hoping he had just mispronounced the word and would realize his mistake.

"Whatever."

"Not whatever, Cheddar—Michael, you do know you're going to Africa, not Australia."

"Whatever. It's all good," he says. "So I flunked geography. It doesn't matter. I am going where you're going. When I imagine my ideal future, like pie-in-the-sky, dream-big, no limits kind of future, I don't see what I am doing for a job or what kind of car I am driving. I just see you, smiling," he says. He looks dead serious.

I don't know what to say to him. Part of me is outraged. He'll be sitting next to me for the next twenty-four hours on the plane. Then a whole two months on the worksite, out in the frigging bush with nothing but the work, the volunteer group, and our village hosts—and who knows what kinds of animals lurking just outside our compound. Then, after that, I'll be stuck with him for a week's tour of South Africa on a minibus.

Part of me also wonders if I deserve such admiration.

But I do know one thing. We will definitely get that school built with Michael Toohey on the job.

ACKNOWLEDGMENTS

Thank you to Thomas Cobb for the encouragement and guidance and Kate Baldwin, Christine Connolly, Marion Fearing, Laura Hentz, Anne-Marie Kennedy, Dean Lunt, Nicole Lussier, Dana and Sam Maguire, Ellen Pekilis, and the team at Islandport Press.

ABOUT THE AUTHOR

A lifelong New Englander, Bee Burke grew up in Rhode Island. She has a BA in Journalism from the University of Rhode Island with a minor in Russian language. She has worked as a reporter, publicist, graphic designer, account executive, travel and fashion copywriter, and editor. When not writing (or at the day job!) Bee can be found vegetable gardening, taking ballet classes, and going on both short and long trips along the coasts of New England and Quebec. Her favorite places include Beavertail Light in Rhode Island, Tadoussac, Quebec, and Campobello Island. Bee is also bossed around by three cats—two tuxedo boys and a cranky torti girl.